Five Nights at Freddy's™

TALES FROM THE PIZZAPLEX

#3 SOMNIPHOBIA

Five Nights at Freddy's™

TALES FROM THE PIZZAPLEX

#3 SOMNIPHOBIA

BY

SCOTT CAWTHON
KELLY PARRA
ANDREA WAGGENER

Scholastic Inc.

Copyright © 2022 by Scott Cawthon. All rights reserved.

Photo of TV static: © Klikk/Dreamstime

All rights reserved. Published by Scholastic Inc., *Publishers since 1920*. SCHOLASTIC and associated logos are trademarks and/or registered trademarks of Scholastic Inc.

The publisher does not have any control over and does not assume any responsibility for author or third-party websites or their content.

No part of this publication may be reproduced, stored in a retrieval system, or transmitted in any form or by any means, electronic, mechanical, photocopying, recording, or otherwise, without written permission of the publisher. For information regarding permission, write to Scholastic Inc., Attention: Permissions Department, 557 Broadway, New York, NY 10012.

This book is a work of fiction. Names, characters, places, and incidents are either the product of the author's imagination or are used fictitiously, and any resemblance to actual persons, living or dead, business establishments, events, or locales is entirely coincidental.

Library of Congress Cataloging-in-Publication Data available

ISBN 978-1-338-83167-2

10 9 8 7 6 5 4 3 2 1   22 23 24 25 26

Printed in the U.S.A.   23

First printing 2022 • Book design by Jeff Shake

TABLE OF CONTENTS

SOMNIPHOBIA

"**I**T'S JUST TERRIBLE, BILL. ALL THESE PEOPLE GAWKING AT THE POOR FAMILY'S BELONGINGS."

Bill eyed his wife. "You mean like we are?"

"Oh hush," Mildred scolded, staring at the display of home items set on several tables at the yard sale. If it gave her something to share at her weekly pinochle game, so be it. "We're concerned neighbors, Bill. Maybe we can take something off their hands so they're able to move on as soon as they can. It's just a shame about Josh. Sweet boy."

Bill scratched his jaw. "Can't say I remember him much."

"Well, he was an odd one. Quiet, kept mostly to himself. And now he's suddenly in a coma, in need of full-time care." She glanced around and added in a loud whisper, "So sad that his parents have to move out of state to get help from their family."

"No rhyme or reason for said coma?"

She picked up a mixing bowl. "One day, he just wouldn't wake up. Doctors called it a medical mystery." Mildred felt a chill and set the bowl back down. The household items suddenly seemed sad and lonely to her. "Maybe we can donate to help out."

Bill picked up a broken sphere with an odd-looking character inside. He assumed it was one of those funny court jesters, wearing a cap and fluffy pants. With a frown, Bill set the ball down. "I think a donation would be best, Milly. Let's go home now."

"Raad, what scares you the most?"

"Cliffs, dude," Raad said. "Or ledges on tall buildings. I get the chills like I might fall over the side. And clowns, definitely. Such a cliché, I know, but I saw some creepy movies as a kid."

Sam Barker listened as he sat with Raad, Jules, Larry, and Bogart in the bleachers at lunch on Friday. It was *the* spot for seniors to hang out. Sam and his friends had been waiting three years to get to this level of the hierarchy. Freshman year, they'd been in the cafeteria. Sophomore year, they sat in the courtyard. Junior year, they ate in front of the school on the steps and now, finally, they were on the bleachers. The only downside, in Sam's opinion, was that the football field attracted the most sunshine.

The sky was clear today, and it was a good thing Sam had applied sunscreen twice before lunch. But as a drip of sweat slid down his forehead, he realized he was going to need to apply a third coat soon in order to not boil like a lobster. With his blond hair and fair skin, he probably should be wearing a hat at lunch from now on just to be safe. He pushed his vintage black-rimmed glasses up his nose and carefully unwrapped his sandwich as he listened to Raad talk about his fears. Yesterday, the lunch topic had been the best films of all time.

"Oh," Raad continued, "and those amusement rides that make you drop from way up high. I feel like my guts get left behind. Sooo not good."

"I love those rides," Bogart announced, and then took a massive bite of his pepperoni pizza slice. Bogart was the most talkative one of the group. He was also the guy who always wore shorts. There hadn't been a day in high school that his calves were covered, even when it was freezing outside.

Jules stood against the side railing as he snacked from a chip bag. He didn't sit often and was usually on the move. Larry chomped on the hamburger and fries that his mom had dropped off for him before lunch. The guys always teased him that his mom still brought him lunch during senior year. Sam had stopped telling him how much trans fat was in those meals when Larry had finally said,

"Bro." Larry was a guy of very few words. His hair was long and frizzy; Sam didn't think he owned a comb.

Raad leaned back on his elbows and had his legs stretched out and crossed in front of him. He wore his clothes two sizes too big but managed to look stylish in them somehow. His white tennis shoes were always clean and bright. Sam wasn't sure how he managed that. He wore his dark hair overgrown so that the ends nearly reached his shoulders. Of course Raad wasn't eating. He usually skipped lunch, no matter how many times Sam told him about the benefits of three meals a day.

Sam was actually surprised his friend was afraid of anything at all. Raad was so easygoing. That was probably why he was able to remain friends with Sam, since everything bothered Sam. Raad had never seemed to pay any mind to his pal's cautious way of life. If Raad hadn't accepted him for who he was since elementary school, Sam felt he likely would have drifted away from the group. Jules, Bogart, and (sometimes) Larry just didn't fully get him.

Sam studied his sandwich—organic turkey, no dairy, on gluten-free bread, with mustard and fresh organic lettuce, tomato, and pickles. He'd made it himself. No way would he eat from the school cafeteria. Who knew how many hands had touched the food prep, how many people were breathing on it. Not only that, but their school district hadn't yet conformed to organic ingredients or no preservatives in their meals.

Sam had researched his upset stomach issues last year and realized gluten, heavy oils, and preservatives didn't sit well with his digestion. His frequent anxiety gave him a nervous stomach. He also had to steer clear of caffeine and sugar or his anxiety shot into overdrive and he couldn't calm down or sleep through the night. He was on a clean, dairy-free, gluten-free, stimulant-free meal plan for the time being. He'd started packing his own meals so he wouldn't have to keep explaining this to his mom.

"Talk about scary. Did you guys hear that Josh's family is moving away with him?" Bogart asked.

"Yeah, bummer all around," Raad said, and cleared his throat. "What about you, Sam? What are the top things you're most afraid of?"

"The world," Jules muttered under his breath.

Bogart snorted.

Sam ignored the comment as he carefully chewed a bite of sandwich before speaking. "I'd say small, confined spaces, definitely the extreme dark, and large bodies of water."

"You mean like the ocean?" Bogart asked.

Sam nodded. "Yeah, I never learned to swim."

"Your dad never taught you?"

Raad looked at Bogart and Bogart adjusted his hat. "Um, I mean—"

"It's okay," Sam said. Everyone knew Sam had lost his dad in third grade. "No, he never taught me."

"I can teach you, Sam," Raad told him.

Sam shook his head. "No thanks. Besides, it's healthy to have fears."

Before the moment could get more awkward, Jules interrupted. "So are we going to Misty's party or what?"

When it came to deciding what the group was going to do it was always *we*. If possible, the group hardly did anything without everyone involved.

"Yeah, I'm in," Raad announced. "Something to do." Then everyone else decided to go, too. Although Sam would rather have stayed home. Parties had stopped being fun sophomore year when everyone stopped playing party games and started worrying what everyone looked like. But he was part of the group, so he was going anyway.

Raad's birthday was Sunday, though, and he'd chosen to hang out at Freddy Fazbear's Mega Pizzaplex to celebrate with the guys. Sam was pretty sure that was going to be more fun than Misty Salazar's party.

Sam walked behind the guys as they entered Misty's house. He wore a freshly ironed collared shirt and dark blue jeans. He always ironed out the wrinkles in his clothes or he felt uncomfortable wearing them. His hair was buzzed short so he never had to style it, and his glasses were freshly polished to a vibrant shine.

The music was loud and there were a ton of kids. Sam didn't especially like big parties. Large parties were attended by the loud kids, the social kids, and often the popular kids. The entire opposite of Sam and his group.

Misty lived in a huge two-story home with a large backyard and swimming pool. That was where most of the partygoers hung out. As Sam followed the guys into the backyard, he made sure to keep a safe distance from the pool. Of course there wasn't a lifeguard in sight. With so many kids there, all kinds of accidents could happen. He shuddered just thinking about the possibilities.

He settled at a table by the fence, positioning himself as far away from the enclosed water as possible. But the scent of chlorine still filled his nostrils. His friends meandered around, talking to other kids. Sam was fine sitting alone. He didn't really talk to other classmates, unless it involved school, and mainly just hung out with his small group of friends. He wasn't the best at small talk, anyway, and he was used to other kids ignoring him or not really being interested in what he had to say.

Sam accepted that he was somewhat of an odd one out in high school. He didn't do sports; he didn't join clubs. He had a specialized diet, and he only wore certain cotton fabrics because polyester made him break out. He was set in his ways and he rarely tried new things. He admittedly considered everything that could go wrong before he decided to do something, instead of thinking of all the things that could go right. But his way of living made him feel comfortable, so he accepted that about himself. It was just that others rarely did. Well, besides Raad.

Surprisingly, a girl named Lydia Gomes walked over to Sam's table. She had curly brown hair, freckles, and a nose piercing. She wore jeans and a colorful sweatshirt. She didn't wear a lot of makeup like some of the girls at Marina High, and she was always nice when Sam had group study with her in English lit.

She held two red cups in her hands. "Hi, Sam. I always wanted to tell you that your glasses are pretty cool. They're so unique."

"Thanks, um, they were my dad's." He adjusted them on his face, even though he didn't need to. It was a nervous habit. "When I needed glasses, my mom put my prescription in them."

"That's really neat. Do you want a drink?" She offered him a cup.

Sam eyed the drink suspiciously. "What is it?"

"Well, I'm told it's Misty's Birthday Poolside Punch."

"Do you know what's in it?"

Lydia frowned at the cups. "Definitely some kind of fruity stuff."

Sam looked around and noticed kids acting silly and talking funny. He held up a hand like a crossing guard. "No thanks, Lydia. If there's even a chance of alcohol being in it, then I'm not having it. I'm a firm believer in staying in control of my mind and my choices."

She gave him a smile. "You sure? A couple of sips won't hurt."

He adjusted his glasses again. "Actually, that's far from true—"

"Sam, just take the drink. Sheesh." Jules was abruptly at the table and grabbed the drink out of Lydia's hand, slapping it down in front of Sam. "Don't mind him. Sam's a glass-half-empty kinda guy . . ."

Sam had been about to explain how alcohol could cause someone to become drowsy and in less control. Instead, Sam cleared his throat. "I make smart and careful decisions in order to navigate around future challenges."

Jules rolled his eyes. "Right."

The rest of the group walked over to the small table. "What's going on, guys?" Raad raised an eyebrow.

"Just Sam being Sam." Jules left it at that and took a big swig from his red cup.

"So have you guys heard about the cliff diving going on in Santa Cruz?" Lydia asked. "I hear it's pretty fun."

"Yeah, a guy I know does it," Bogart jumped in. "Says it's an extreme rush. You gotta love heights, though. Guess that leaves you out, Raad."

"No doubt," Raad said.

"One day, I'd like to try it," Lydia said.

Sam shook his head. "People have actually broken their necks and other body parts from reckless jumps off cliffs and bridges. Not long ago there was an incident on the news about a guy that did a cliff dive. The cliff was so high up that he couldn't control where he landed. He ended up falling on a bunch of rocks, breaking every single one of his bones, and splitting open his skull. They said his brain was eaten by the birds when they found him."

"Dude."

"That's *gnarly.*"

"True story. I'd definitely steer clear of that activity, Lydia," Sam warned.

"Um, okay," Lydia said, and looked around the backyard. "Oh, I see my friend. Talk to you guys later." Then she took off rather quickly.

"Good one, Sam," Jules blurted as Lydia rushed away. "Real smooth."

"What do you mean?"

"You really impressed Lydia with your death talk."

"She should be impressed. Making safe choices in order to have a secure and long life span is a plus."

Jules made a sound like a buzzer. "More like a negative with your doom-and-gloom attitude."

Sam frowned. "I don't have a negative attitude."

"No? Why wouldn't you take the drink?"

"I don't like to be uninhibited."

"Whatever that means. Why are you sitting so far from the pool?"

"You know I can't swim. Are you aware of how many accidents happen in home pools?"

"What's the leading cause of death in the US?"

"Well, that's easy. Heart disease."

Jules threw his arms up, spilling some of his drink on the ground. "I rest my case! You're a walking encyclopedia for doom and gloom!"

"All right, Jules," Raad cut in. "Chill." He patted Sam on the back. "No worries, Sam. It's all good. Let's all just relax and have some fun."

Sam nodded his head even though Jules was making him feel bad. Maybe high school girls didn't understand Sam, but at least he had one good friend who did.

Jules must not have liked what Raad had said, or maybe he had had too much to drink, because he took the cup Lydia had brought for Sam and shoved it in Sam's face. "Here, Sam. Some of this will help you relax."

Sam attempted to block Jules's hand, but the drink splashed into Sam's mouth and down his shirt anyway.

Sam quickly stood and pushed Jules away. The cup fell to the ground, spilling the liquid into a small puddle. He tasted the artificial sourness of the drink, spat it out on the ground, then swiped at his mouth with the back of his hand.

Jules and Bogart laughed.

"Oh shoot," Bogart muttered, with a hand over his mouth. "You've really done it this time, Jules."

Sam blinked rapidly. The disgusting taste of the drink lingered in his mouth, and he didn't know what was in it. He didn't like the taste. He didn't like to be taken out of his comfort zone. And sometimes, he just didn't like Jules.

"Jules, not cool," Raad said. "You okay, Sam?"

"No. *No.*" Sam shook his head as he stalked into the house, searching for water to get the bad taste out of his mouth and to clean his shirt. His breaths became uneven and he knew his anxiety had kicked in. There was a pressure building in the center of his chest. His hands started to clench and unclench as he pushed through kids, trying to get to the kitchen. He opened the fridge and found a water bottle, quickly opening it to drink some and swish it around his mouth before spitting it into the sink. He could feel kids staring at him, but he didn't care. He just needed to calm down and regain control. He pulled off a paper towel from the roll and poured some water on it and then dabbed at his shirt. The drink had stained it a weird blue color. It was likely ruined.

Sam started to sweat, and he couldn't stop blinking. His entire body felt stiff with tension.

He needed to change. His shirt was dirty and wet.

He felt like the party, the kids, were closing in on him.

He wanted out. *Needed* out.

He tossed the paper towel, stomped through the party, and exited through the front door.

The long walk home and the cool air against his face would calm him down. It usually did.

"Sam went home, Raad," Bogart told him. "Saw him leave out the front door."

Raad nodded. Even though he hadn't been the one to upset Sam, he felt bad for what went down. He felt bad for Sam a lot. "He probably just needed some time to cool off."

"What's the big deal?" Jules asked. "It was a joke. I joke with people all the time. You don't see anyone else throwing temper tantrums."

"It wasn't that funny, Jules. Especially to Sam."

Jules snorted. "Why does he have to act all weird? He's always so uptight with his *don't do this, don't do that* attitude. The guy needs to loosen up. He's always spreading his potential doom around. I get tired of it. You too, right, Bogart? Larry?"

Bogart shrugged and looked down at the ground. "I don't know."

Larry shook his head. "Bro."

"Right," Jules muttered, giving them both an irritated look.

Raad shrugged a shoulder. "Sam's different. We're all different in our own ways. No one's perfect. You got to accept people for who they are, Jules. I accept you, don't I?"

When Jules didn't say anything, Raad just said, "Let's bail." He was no longer in a partying mood.

On the day of Raad's birthday, the Mega Pizzaplex was packed. There were long lines for Monty's Gator Golf, Roxy's Raceway, and Fazer Blast, but the guys had waited them out and got their play time in. Glamrock Freddy and Roxanne Wolf walked around the mall area greeting children. Sam could hear mechanical sounds as the characters moved, and he wondered if there were people inside the costumes or if they really were animatronics.

The scents of pizza, popcorn, and cotton candy filled the air. Sam figured they piped those smells through the air to get more sales, and sure enough every other kid held a fluffy ball of cotton candy and a bag of greasy popcorn. Sam tried not to shudder.

Chatter filled every inch of the space. People were talking. Kids were yelling and parents were scolding. Someone laughed really loud. Music played from all directions. It was sensory overload. And not just the sounds: Neon lights glowed throughout the entertainment mall, giving the place a futuristic feel. Visiting the Mega Pizzaplex felt like being inside a video game.

"I'm telling you, guys," Raad said to them as he guided them through the crowd toward the Fazcade prize shop. "All I want is one of Moondrop's Dream Spheres. If we put all our winning tickets together, I bet we can get one.

It'd be a cool birthday gift." He pointed to the boxed ball on the shelf.

"What is it exactly?" Jules asked, eyeing the packaged sphere.

Sam hadn't spoken to Jules since the incident at Misty Salazar's party, and Jules had given him some space. They'd been through these incidents in the past, and if they ignored them, things would slowly go back to normal. However, Sam knew nothing was ever truly resolved between them. It would likely all happen again until Sam stood up to Jules. Since Sam tried to avoid all confrontation, the cycle would likely continue.

"It helps you study," Raad told them. "It lights the room up and helps you slip into a hypnotic state in order to focus better. It supposedly takes information from your subconscious and brings it more clearly into view. You guys gotta help me. If I don't pass physics, I'll be stuck in summer school."

Sam eyed the box. The dream sphere appeared to be a snow globe with Moondrop the jester inside. Half the character's face was a pale crescent moon; the other half was eclipsed in darkness. He wore a cap and puffy blue pants decorated in stars and a gray top with a frilly collar. Bells hung from his hat, both wrists, and tips of his shoes.

"It's a thousand tickets," Sam said. "How much do we have saved up?"

"Seven hundred and ninety," Bogart answered. The guys always pooled their tickets, and Bogart was the official ticket holder. They'd figured they would eventually save up enough tickets all together to get a really cool prize they might all be able to use.

Sam was determined to get the dream sphere for Raad since he was such a good friend. And hey, Sam had a big test coming up, so maybe he'd give it try. *If* it was safe.

For the next hour, the guys all played the high-ticket arcade games. Sam liked to play games where the light spun around a big circle of numbers and you had to hit the button to try to get the biggest ticket prize. He'd landed on some 10s, 22, and then 40. A handful of tokens later, he topped off the ticket wins by scoring a 100-ticket jackpot!

"Way to go, Sam!" Raad praised.

"That was pure luck," Jules muttered.

"All right," Bogart said once he collected Sam's tickets. "I think that put us at the mark. Let's go get this dream sphere."

The guys went to the prize area to wait in the line. While they waited, Jules and Bogart poked fun at some of the adults and kids.

"Oh, dude, look at the shirt on that guy. It's like two sizes too small," Bogart said. "His big belly's hanging out."

Jules, Bogart, and Larry all snickered, but Sam and Raad didn't care for that form of entertainment. When it was finally their turn at the counter, the girl at the prize register took all their tickets from the backpack and dumped them into a bucket to be counted by the machine.

"One thousand and one. What do you guys want?" she asked them.

"The Moondrop's Dream Sphere for the birthday boy, please," Bogart told her.

The guys all laughed at that for some reason.

The girl grabbed the boxed sphere and handed it over to Raad. "Have fun," she said with a smile and tossed her hair over her shoulder. The girls always tended to gravitate toward Raad. "And happy birthday."

"Thanks," he said with a smile.

The dream sphere was in blue-and-black packaging, with neon letters spelling out: MOONDROP'S DREAM SPHERE. Up close, Sam could see Moondrop had an odd-looking grin and a pointy nose.

Raad was pleased. "All right! Thanks, guys. This is so cool. Let's head to my house and take this thing for a test run."

The Dawsons' house was pretty roomy now that two of Raad's siblings were away at college, but it still felt full of family. Raad had a cousin who was never far from his mother, his grandparents stayed over on the weekends, and he had a string of aunts, uncles, and cousins that visited often.

Sometimes Sam wondered what it felt like to belong to such a huge family. Sam was an only child, just like his parents. His only grandparents lived out of state. Since his dad died, it was just Mom and Sam for holidays and special occasions. Although, since his mom was an art teacher, she always had a school event to attend or to volunteer for. Sam had spent most of his teen years helping out at carnivals, dances, and fundraisers.

Raad's parents had left a note that they were out buy-ing his cake. As the guys settled in the living room, Sam read aloud the fine print on the dream sphere box. "Warning: Only use Moondrop's Dream Sphere for ten minutes a day." Sam frowned. "I wonder why?"

"Don't know, but that's what we'll do," Raad told him. "You can time it for us. Get your study notes, guys, and prepare to be hypnotized." Now Sam understood why Raad had asked them to bring their notebooks to his house before heading to the Mega Pizzaplex.

Raad took the box from Sam and removed the sphere. The sphere was set on a black platform with a button to turn it on and off. Raad plugged in the device and set it on the coffee table.

Brutus, Raad's dog, wagged his tail as he waddled into the room. He was a big brown Catahoula mix with a spiked red collar because Raad's mom thought it looked cute. If a dog named Brutus could ever, really, be referred to as *cute*.

Raad knelt down and rubbed the dog's big head as a thick line of drool hung from Brutus's wide mouth. "How ya doing, boy?" Brutus began to happily lick Raad's face.

Sam adjusted his glasses. "My dad told me this story once when I was little. He had a good friend in college. They went to parties and all that. One night the guy got pretty smashed and he fell asleep on his friend's couch. They had a dog. That morning he woke up and the dog had eaten his face off."

"Ooooh!"

"Bro."

"That's sick!"

Raad frowned, looking a little disturbed. He patted his dog's head before pushing Brutus back. "That's enough for you, big boy."

Sam nodded matter-of-factly. "True story. So I'm wary of dogs."

"You want to know what I'm wary of?" Bogart asked. "Guinea pigs. My cousin Howie had one. He liked to feed him carrots. One day, he looks away for a second— chomp! The guinea bites off the tip of his pinky thinking it was a baby carrot."

"All right, guys," Raad says with a shake of his head. "Let's get back to the dream sphere, please."

Sitting on the couch, Larry studied the sphere. "This dream sphere isn't going to really work, is it?"

"You're starting to sound like Sam," Jules said in an annoyed tone.

"Truth?" Bogart said. "I'll try about anything that helps get me out of real studying."

"Are we sure this is safe?" Sam asked Raad.

"Come on, Sam, what could go wrong with a spinning globe with lights?"

"Seizures, but only in some people with epilepsy. Otherwise, I guess not much."

"Oh, that's pretty rich coming from Captain Doom and Gloom," Jules said.

Sam felt the room tense. It was a little too early to go back to teasing when the party incident was still fresh.

"Let's try it," Raad said, breaking the silence. "I'll

even put Brutus outside so he can't eat our faces off while we're hypnotized."

Bogart snorted and Larry smiled.

Putting Brutus outside was smart thinking, Sam thought. "Okay, then, let me set my watch alarm for ten minutes."

"Hey, Brutus, where's your toy?" Brutus looked around the room and grabbed a big, chewed-up rope and brought it to Raad.

"He certainly likes to chew on things," Sam observed.

"Time to play outside, boy," Raad told Brutus and took him out of the room.

When Raad came back, the guys were all seated on the couches and chairs around the coffee table, notebooks open on their laps.

"Let's do this, Moondrop!" Bogart yelled. "Make me smarter!"

"If that's even physically possible," Jules said with a smirk.

"Only time will tell."

"All right, ready, guys? Here we go." Raad pushed the ON button and Sam started the timer on his watch. The lights glowed out of the dream sphere, shining on the walls and ceiling. Moondrop turned in a circle, waving his hands. The jester's eyes glowed red. Shining lights flashed across everyone's faces.

At first, Sam didn't feel any different. The lights were just annoying and made him blink. But in the next moment, a light-headed feeling came over him. He lifted his hand and he moved slowly, as if the air was heavy and thick like syrup. He was aware of his friends, but they seemed far away, as if the room had stretched really wide.

"Do you guys feel that?" Bogart murmured.

"So cool," Jules said.

"Whoooooa," Larry said.

Words began to float off the notebooks and into the air around them.

"Guys," Raad said in awe. "Look at that."

The notes transformed from words and numbers into pictures that surrounded them. The ceiling faded away and was replaced by a blue sky and a bright, shining sun. They were standing on sand dunes with the Pyramids of Giza nearby. The sun beat down on them and the heat was scorching.

"It's hot here," someone said.

"Look at the structure of the pyramids."

"Hey, this is from my world history notes."

Sam could no longer tell who was speaking. The words might have even come from him. It was as if their voices had all become deeply monotone.

"Wow."

"It's like lucid dreaming."

"This is unbelievable."

"Dude, I'm, like, seriously in Egypt."

The pyramids faded away, and a huge airplane was taking off on a runway. The guys ducked as the plane lifted over their heads. They were in awe as the harsh sound of the plane vibrated above them. A kinematic equation involving the airplane's distance before takeoff drifted across their eyes.

The room turned into a warm restaurant kitchen with stainless steel countertops and a large brick oven. A cook took a pepperoni pizza out of the oven. Sam could even smell the pepperoni as the cook began to cut the pizza into fractions.

"Can I eat that pizza?"

"I'm hungry again."

"Yum."

A girl in a Renaissance-era dress stood on a balcony, shouting, "O Romeo, Romeo . . ."

"Ah, man, who brought their English literature?"

"I didn't bring my *Romeo and Juliet* notes. I think it's picking up on stuff we learned in class."

"This is getting trippy."

Sam's wristwatch began to beep with a distant echo.

"You guys hear that? Time to shut off the dream sphere."

Suddenly, the lights on the sphere shut off. Moondrop went still, and the guys sat for a moment in the unexpected quiet. They stared at one another and then Raad said, "That was the coolest thing I've ever experienced."

The group started laughing together.

"I can't believe it worked!" Bogart said. "I felt like I was literally in another world."

"That was awesome," said Jules. "I remember everything! The facts, the equations. It's like I'm experiencing a photographic memory right now."

"Cool," said Larry.

"I feel really good," Sam added in awe. "Like I could

learn anything and everything in a matter of minutes. I'm surprised that this worked. Amazed, actually."

"This is the best birthday present, guys," Raad said. "Thanks. I am so passing all my classes this year. We have to do this every week. I'll even share the wealth. One of us can take it home for a week and then someone else the next week. This is too fantastic to keep all to myself."

Sam's hand went straight up before anyone could say anything. "I'll take it first." He was almost surprised at how fast he volunteered. But there was something really exciting about the dream sphere. It made him feel something he hadn't felt in years. He wasn't sure if it was excitement, or eagerness, or even something freeing about it. He just knew he wanted to do it again.

"I guess Sam wants the dream sphere superbad," Bogart said with a laugh.

"Figures," Jules muttered.

Bogart adjusted his hat. "All I know is that after seeing the pizza guy, I could eat more pizza. In fact, I could win a pizza-eating contest . . ."

"Binge eating isn't safe," Sam told him. "I once read about a kid who was in a hot dog–eating contest. He ate so many in twenty minutes that he suffocated. When they opened him up, his stomach and intestines were packed so tight with the links that the hot dogs had slipped into his airways. It took literally days to get all the hot dogs out."

Jules rolled his eyes.

"Sick," Larry said.

"Sam, you need to lay off the crazy stories," Bogart suggested.

"Anyways"—Raad unplugged the dream sphere and handed it to Sam—"The sphere's all yours, bud. We'll trade next week."

Sam took the sphere and smiled. This week was going to be awesome. Then he realized something strange. He could have sworn the sphere vibrated in his hands, ever so slightly.

Sam heard rock music blaring from his mom's bedroom. Mom was painting again.

"Sam? You home?" he heard her call out.

"Yeah, Mom, I'm home," he yelled back. "I brought you food from Raad's party." He set the foil-covered plate on the breakfast bar.

Sam and his mom lived in a two-bedroom, one-bathroom apartment. The bedrooms and living area were large, and with just the two of them it was a comfortable home. Mom's art brought color to the space. The walls were bright blue and covered in her vibrant paintings. The living room couch was a rustic orange layered with a cozy blanket and fancy pillows. There were a few family pictures on the television stand with Dad, Mom, and him. The kitchen had a mini breakfast bar off the counter and a small island in the center of the kitchen area.

The music cut off and his mom strolled in from her bedroom. Her blonde hair was bundled on top of her head. She had blue paint on her cheek and she wore a paint-splattered smock. She was wiping her hands with a colorful stained rag.

"How was *Raad's* party?" she asked. "Was it totally *rad*?"

"Mom, when are you going to stop saying Raad's name like that?"

"Oh, I'd say in about a hundred years, when it finally gets old."

"It's way past its expiration date."

"Hmm. Well, I made cupcakes. Want one?"

Sam lifted his eyebrows. "Are they gluten-free with an unprocessed sweetener?"

"They are not gluten-free, and they are made with absolutely delicious processed sugar and chocolate."

He shook his head. "No thanks. I'll pass."

"Guess I'll be sharing them in the teachers' lounge."

"Mom, you knew I wouldn't have any."

"I dream of the day when you'll wake up and smell the sugar."

Sam placed the dream sphere on the breakfast bar next to the plate.

His mom walked over to the sphere. "And what is *that* thing?"

"It's a dream sphere. It helps you study. We won it at the Mega Pizzaplex for Raad, and we're each taking turns using it."

His mom picked up the sphere and shifted it in her hands, watching Moondrop turn left and right. "He's a weird-looking little guy. Helps you study, huh? How about helps you to kick crazy diets and encourages you to eat pizza, cake, and candy like a normal teenager?"

"Mom, my digestion is fifty percent better on my new meal plan, and I'm more energized, if you haven't noticed. It's the new me."

Mom made a show of staring at his face. "Nope. Still the same kiddo to me. Handsome as ever, though."

"Sure, Mom." Sam shook his head, but he was used to his mom's jokes. She was one of the strongest people he'd ever met. She'd somehow worked through the grief of losing her high school sweetheart and helped Sam through grieving over his father at such a young age while still managing to help them survive. His dad had been the breadwinner in the family while his mom took care of him and followed her dream of being a full-time artist. Her paintings hadn't really taken off, but her passion never faded, even when she had to go back to work as a middle school art teacher. She had to squeeze in moments to paint for herself nowadays. Sam didn't feel so bad hanging out with his friends when his mom was alone. It gave her a chance to paint.

"Thanks for bringing me the food," Mom said. "Smells yummy."

"There's birthday cake, too."

"Double the sugar and gluten for me. Even better."

The next day after school, Sam set up Moondrop's Dream Sphere in his room. His mom always stayed a little longer at her school to get things prepared for the following day, and he had some time to himself. He'd placed the dream sphere on his bedside table and plugged the cord into a nearby wall outlet.

Like the living room, his mom made sure his bedroom was accented with color. His walls were forest green, with light wooden furnishings. She'd bought him light brown bedding with highlights of dark blue and green. His tall bookshelf was lined with some of his favorite childhood books and a few toys that his dad had bought him. He also had a ton of books on digestion, health, germs, and making smart choices. His favorite picture of him and his dad sat on the top shelf. They were sitting on his dad's motorcycle, probably about to go on one of their father-and-son rides.

Sam sat on his bed and picked up a two-subject notebook with school notes on English literature and ocean science. He set his wristwatch alarm for ten minutes. He decided to take off his glasses and set them on the little table and then he pushed the button to start the dream sphere.

Moondrop turned, and the lights flashed across Sam's face. After a moment, he began to feel that slow, heavy feeling sink over his body. It felt so surreal that he wondered what would happen if he stood up, but he didn't want to chance falling over and hurting himself. Words floated out of the notebook, dancing before him and then fading into the air.

First, he appeared right in the middle of *Hamlet*. The costumes were straight out of a historical text. The words from the performers were spoken naturally. He felt as if he was witnessing William Shakespeare's imagination at play right in his mind.

Sam went to adjust his glasses and remembered he took

them off. Then it dawned on him. He actually could see very clearly without wearing his glasses while using the dream sphere. "That's cool," he murmured.

He was thrust into the ocean, and before Sam could panic, he realized he could actually walk and breathe underwater! He floated down to the ocean floor and glided across the sand and rock, careful not to step on any crawling sea creatures. He sensed the coldness of the water, but it wasn't overwhelming. A school of fish scattered away as a pod of humpback whales swam close by, singing a song. Though even in a dream state, his mind specified that humpback whales' songs were made up of groans, grunts, and whistles most of the time. Seahorses floated past him. A sea turtle slowly swam below the whales. Then the whales swam by Sam, and the most peaceful feeling came over him. He reached out a hand and touched one of the whales. He could have sworn the eye of the whale actually looked at him. The songs of the whales seemed to glide through the ripples of water.

Suddenly, his wristwatch sounded, and a sense of loss overcame Sam as he pulled back from the lucid experience. It was an odd shift from dream reality into his present. He pushed the button on the dream sphere to turn it off and clicked off his alarm. But as he adapted once again to the surroundings of his bedroom, a smile spread across his face.

"That was fantastic!" he yelled out.

Sam jumped up and did a little dance as he looked at himself in the mirror. He could admit it was odd to see such a full smile on his face. It really transformed him. He hardly ever smiled, and for once he could admit that he looked and *felt* happy. He even flexed his arms and wondered if he should start lifting some weights. He did the cardio that was recommended to maintain a healthy lifestyle, but maybe he should add to it. He'd definitely think on that.

Sam's stomach growled. He was so energized that he got the idea to treat his mom to a homemade dinner. He slipped his glasses back on and went to the kitchen to cook one of her favorite dishes.

An hour later, when his mom came home, her eyes widened in surprise. "Have I walked into the wrong apartment?"

Sam smiled. "Nope. This is your home, with your son, making you your favorite gluten-and-processed-cheese lasagna."

"Be still, my heart. Sam, what has brought this on?"

Sam knew it was the dream sphere, but . . . "I just felt good and I wanted to show my appreciation for all the things you do for me. So I cooked you dinner and I even had time to straighten up the apartment."

Mom's mouth popped open. "You cleaned the bathroom?"

Sam squinted at her. "I'm not feeling *that* good."

"Of course not." Mom walked over and put a hand to his face. "You don't seem warm. You sure you're feeling okay?"

Sam shrugged her hand off. "Mom, stop, I feel fine. Just trying to do something nice."

She smiled. "Sam, thank you. I appreciate the gesture. This looks wonderful. Let me change and then we can eat. What are you going to have?"

He popped open the oven. "I also have one gluten-free lasagna minus the cheese."

She laughed. "I'll be ready in five."

The next day, Sam eyed the dream sphere in his bedroom. While at school, he'd replayed his session from the day before over and over in his mind. It had felt surreal and yet so real. It was like he traveled to other worlds right from the confines of his bedroom. He *really* wanted to extend the experience just a little bit longer.

"I bet it would be fine to go for, say, fifteen minutes," he reasoned, adjusting his glasses. "It's only five minutes more. Shouldn't really make a difference. I mean, what could it hurt?"

He didn't have any new notes from school to study, so he sat with his entire government book, which was pretty thick. He set his wristwatch to fifteen minutes, removed his glasses, and, with a push of the button, turned on the dream sphere.

Moondrop began to turn, and the lights from the sphere flashed across Sam's face. The notes of the book floated through the air and the branches of the government moved across his eyes. He witnessed the Declaration of Independence being signed, followed by the historical timeline for voting rights. He watched George Washington take the oath to become the first president and was in awe viewing the parade of US presidents who followed as they were sworn into office. He witnessed treaties and laws being passed. He glimpsed wars being fought, which upset him, and then finally it was as if the entire contents of the book had slipped into his mind like a human computer downloading a file.

"Whoa." He was starting to feel like some kind of genius with so much knowledge packed in his brain. He felt himself tremble from the intensity and the amount of information he had witnessed. Maybe, he considered, the entire government book was a little too much.

In the next moment, the scene changed and he found himself at a small park.

This is strange, he thought. *Could this park be part of the history in the book?*

His wristwatch began to beep that his time was up.

But Sam waited a moment longer before clicking off the dream sphere. The park looked slightly familiar. It could be any park, really, with a sandbox, slide, swing set, and seesaw. Tall trees were scattered around. It was a nice day with only a few clouds in the sky. Birds were chirping and other kids played in the sandbox and on the swings. But then he saw . . .

"Hey, bud, let's play tag. You're it."

"Dad?" Sam said, and the one word seemed to echo around him.

Beep . . . beep . . .

Yeah, this park was part of history. Sam's history.

"Come on, catch me!" His dad smiled. He was young and healthy, just like Sam remembered him. He had overgrown light-brown hair with some scruff on his face from not shaving for a few days. He wore faded jeans, black work boots, and a T-shirt. He was wearing his signature Ray-Bans. He waved Sam to come after him, and then Sam jogged toward him.

But Sam was little, and his dad had always been faster.

"Dad, wait, you're too fast!"

"Come on, catch me. That's the game!"

Then Sam lost him.

He was gone.

Sam looked around, a little nervous. "Dad? Where are you?"

He spotted something blue and gray shift at the corner of his eye. Sam turned to see what it was, but he saw nothing but a few trees.

Suddenly, his dad jumped out from behind a tree in front of him. "Gotcha!"

"You scared me!"

They both laughed really hard as his dad picked him up and swung him around in a big circle.

Beep . . . beep . . . beep.

Sam pulled himself back from the memory and hesitantly switched off the dream sphere and then his watch alarm.

He was still laughing.

Until he was crying.

He sat there in the quiet for a long time, experiencing the lost memory over and over again in his mind.

Sam was searching in the hall closet, digging through old boxes. It was their junk drawer, full of sentimental items, as well as odd things they didn't always need but occasionally used, like superglue, masking tape, a screwdriver, a hammer, an old paint roller, and a wrench. He was pretty sure the wrench was his dad's and would never be used again in this lifetime.

"Sam, what are you looking for?" Mom asked from behind him.

Sam's nose itched from the dust, and he sneezed once. Then again.

"Twice, three times for the gold!" his mom announced dramatically.

He rubbed at his nose. "I was just looking for some of Dad's things."

"Oh, what do you need?"

"I don't know. I want to remember him." Sam pulled out a box of photo albums and old yearbooks, then shoved it back.

There was a pause, and then Mom said, "Grab that white box with the removable lid on the top shelf."

Sam grabbed the box and brought it to the living room.

Mom had her hands on her hips. "What made you want to look at your father's stuff?"

Sam shrugged. "I had a memory and I thought it would be nice to remember some more."

"What was the memory?"

Sam's lips curved. "We were at some park, playing tag. I could never catch him."

Mom smiled back. "Yeah, it would always tire you out, running around after your dad." Together, they sat on the couch and lifted the lid. "These are a few of your dad's things." She took out a wallet, faded and worn-out on the edges, and the keys to his motorcycle, though the bike had been totaled in the accident. There was a favorite white shirt of his that had a hole in the collar, a few collectable coins, and some old pictures from when Dad was a little kid.

"You look like him when he was younger," Sam's mom said.

Sam could see the familial resemblance in the nose, shape of the face, and mouth. "Wow, I never realized that I kind of look like him."

There were also a bunch of CDs with a portable CD player and headphones.

"Dad loved music like you do," Sam recalled. "I forgot about that."

Mom sighed. "Yeah, I have most of the old CDs in my room, but here are some of his other ones that he liked as a teenager."

Sam studied the CD cases. Lots of rock-and-roll bands and a few solo artists. He pulled out the CD player with headphones. "Can I use this?"

"Sure, honey. Take what you need. There are some new batteries in the drawer in the kitchen. Your dad would have liked you to listen to his old favorites."

Sam took some of the CDs and put the box back in the closet. After he replaced the batteries in the player, he went to his room and shut the door. He put a CD into the portable player and slipped on the headphones as he lay down on his bed.

Slow rock music played, and he closed his eyes, thinking of his dad.

In government class, Sam was handed back his latest test. "Excellent work, Sam," Mr. Taylor praised him. "You're at the top of the grading curve now. I'm glad to see you putting more effort into your studies."

Sam nodded with a smile. "Thanks, Mr. Taylor." He'd aced the test and the extra credit questions with a total score of 115 percent. He usually scored in the 90s. So he'd definitely upped his grade with the help of the dream sphere.

Jules leaned toward him from the desk next to him. "When are you gonna share the sphere?"

Sam adjusted his glasses. "After the week's over. I've only had it a couple of days."

"You already aced the test. It's my turn now."

"We made a plan, Jules. We've got to stick to it."

Jules frowned. "It's not like it's *your* sphere."

Sam shifted uncomfortably in his seat. "Talk to Raad. It was his idea, and it's his dream sphere."

Jules sat back with a scowl, and Sam took a steady breath. He didn't realize his pulse was speeding up. He had a few more days with the sphere and then one of the other guys would take it home. That was the plan, and it wasn't going to be a problem. Well, he didn't think it would be a problem.

He was so caught up in thinking about the sphere that it took him a moment to realize he hadn't let Jules push him around.

Raad caught up with Sam as he walked to the bleachers for lunch.

"How's it going with the dream sphere?" Raad asked.

"Pretty good," Sam said, slipping on the hat he had remembered to bring this week. "I'm taking in a lot of notes. I aced my latest government test." He didn't mention the memory of his dad. It was too private, too personal, and while Raad was his good friend, he felt more comfortable talking about his dad with his mom.

"That's cool. I'm glad it's working out for you. Hey, are you doing anything after school tomorrow?"

"Don't think so. Why?"

"My dad asked me to do some yard work and trim this old tree we have in the backyard. I could use some help if you're up for it."

Sam nodded. "Oh sure. I'll be there."

"Thanks. With two of us, we'll get it done in no time." Raad hesitated. "And look, Sam, I'm sorry Jules gave you a hard time at Misty's party."

"You have nothing to apologize about. It wasn't you. It was just Jules being Jules."

"You're both my friends, you know?"

Sam nodded. "Yeah, I get it."

The friends left it at that as they climbed up the bleachers to meet with the rest of the group.

Sometimes Sam hung with the guys after school and joked around for half an hour, but today he went straight home. He was eager to use the dream sphere again. Eager to feel good. Eager to feel energized. Eager for another lucid experience.

He grabbed an apple, washed it, and then took it to his bedroom. He had a few notes from one subject to use and, well, he wondered if another memory might pop up.

A memory of his dad.

He occasionally dreamed of his dad, but the dream always faded when he awoke. Sometimes he looked at pictures to remember him, but it wasn't the same as the vivid memory he'd experienced. It had been like he was really reliving that fun moment at the park when he was little. Back then, there hadn't been a care in the world. There'd been laughter, fun, and joy. Feeling joyful and carefree wasn't really part of his life anymore and that was kind of sad when he thought about it.

It's not that he didn't love his mom, but with Dad gone, there was a hole in their family that never seemed to be filled. When he experienced the vivid memory, that hole had been briefly filled and overflowing.

He wanted to experience it all again.

He took a bite of his apple and set his watch to fifteen minutes, then hesitated. When he'd last used the sphere, the lucid dream of his dad hadn't come until after the first fifteen minutes of study time.

Five minutes more hadn't seemed to hurt him. "I'm sure ten minutes more would be just fine, too," he said. There was a familiar voice in the back of his mind telling him it might not be such a good idea, but he squashed it. He couldn't always be Captain Doom.

He might have a full five minutes of time with his dad in the dream state. When he'd went over a couple of minutes past fifteen, he'd felt fine. In fact, he felt fantastic each time he used the dream sphere. Even better than being on his gluten-free meal plan. He took a breath and reset his watch alarm for twenty minutes.

When he slipped off his glasses, he pushed the dream sphere's ON button. The lights spun, the heavy feeling sunk into his body, and the study notes came alive. He experienced ocean science on a new level. He could feel that the oceans were very old. Ancient. Billions of years of history could be told through the oceans. But Sam hesitated to take in that much information. He had a sudden thought that his mind couldn't handle it all. Then the scene shifted.

The apple he'd been eating floated up into the air. It broke apart in sections of the stem, the core, the seeds, the inner pulp of the apple, and the skin.

The nutrients of the apple listed before his eyes, as well as the health benefits to the body.

"Wow," he said in awe. "Looks like I need to eat more apples."

Then the memories arrived.

His mom and dad took him on a road trip to an amusement park. They rode fast rides, played games, and ate funnel cake. Dad won him a stuffed giraffe and let him sit on his shoulders as they walked through the swarm of people. He could see everything from that height. He thought he saw a funny hat with a bell hanging from the tip among the crowd and a clown with fluffy red hair up ahead of them. He could feel the light brush of wind against his skin from that day. A seagull flew by him and landed on a nearby fence. Sam tried to grab it. The bird squawked and flew away.

A trip to the zoo followed. Dad kneeled down next to Sam, and they watched the gorillas stretch out in the sun. He could smell his dad's aftershave and felt the comfort of being with him. The smaller monkeys made Sam laugh as they swung from trees and picked at one another's hair. His dad tried to pick at his hair, and they giggled together.

There was a fun moment when they had a picnic at the beach. Mom and Dad helped him make sandcastles molded with plastic buckets, but a wave washed them over. Sam was upset until his dad splashed him with cold seawater and a splash fight began. Sam could taste the salty air as if he was really there and feel the grainy sand on his skin.

He relived family movie night. Sam sat on the couch, squeezed in between Mom and Dad with a big bowl of popcorn on his lap. His mouth watered with the taste of butter, and his skin warmed at the coziness of the room. He felt loved and secure, wedged in the middle of his parents.

Those were some of the best moments of his life.

It seemed Sam had forgotten all the wonderful times they'd had together. Or perhaps he had buried them deep within his mind because remembering had hurt too much.

His alarm sounded. Sam turned off the dream sphere with a soft smile on his face. He wasn't too sad this time. He was content to relive those moments again. He pulled out the CD player, slipped on the headphones, and lay back on his bed, listening to his dad's music. Then he replayed the memories he'd just experienced in his mind like his own personal home movie.

Sometime later, he blinked when he heard his mom come into the apartment. His room had slightly darkened with the late afternoon. He sat up, pulled off the headphones, and rubbed at his eyes, trying to shake the drowsy feeling from his head. He looked at his watch. He'd been lying down replaying the memories in his mind for over an hour and a half. He hadn't even realized how much time had passed.

That evening, Sam found his mom in his room holding the dream sphere.

A flash of irritation came over him. "Mom, what are you doing?" His voice was urgent, and he tried to stop himself from snatching it away from her.

Mom's eyes widened. "Whoa, just checking out the funny ball. What's got you in a twist?"

He adjusted his glasses. "Nothing. I didn't know what you were doing. It's Raad's. We have to be careful with it. Please just leave it alone."

"I know it's Raad's. Sheesh. Have you been using this every day?"

"No," he fibbed, crossing his arms. "But, when I do, it helps me to remember my school notes."

Mom lifted her eyebrow. "Hmm. I don't recall you every having trouble memorizing your notes before. And you seem to be a little intense about this ball."

Sam blinked. "What? I'm not intense."

She gave him the Mom stare that he knew so well. A look that basically said, "Get real." "Just be careful with things like these, Sam. Pretty soon, you could be clucking like a chicken, and then what would we do? And I'm only half kidding."

Sam sighed. "Sure, Mom."

She finally set the sphere down and left his room, closing the door behind her. Sam felt his heartbeat start to slow down.

He sat on his bed and picked up the sphere. Moondrop stared up at him with his red eyes. "If she only knew how truly great you are, she wouldn't be giving me a hard time about you."

He felt a strange vibration coming from the sphere again and felt the urge to give the dream sphere another go even though he'd already had a session that day. *Maybe just a quick ten minutes*, he thought.

But when he heard his mom washing the dishes and singing along with the radio, he decided to wait until tomorrow. He might be too distracted with his mom at home.

During the night, he tossed and turned. He could sense the sphere sitting beside him on the little table. He didn't look at it, but he knew it was there. The sheets felt itchy and warm. He kicked off a sheet and rolled to the side. Moondrop stared right at him. For a split second, he thought the red eyes flashed bright.

He blinked, and the light was gone. He was probably just half asleep. But he still felt that uncomfortable urge to turn on the dream sphere and to slip back into that familiar lucid state.

He reached out his hand to push the ON button and again stopped himself.

Sam blinked rapidly in irritation, and his chest felt tight. He clicked on the table lamp and sat up in bed, picking up the dream sphere. His shoulders were stiff, and his legs were restless. He couldn't relax. But with the sphere, he always felt calm. He really needed that right now.

He shook his head. "No. I can wait until tomorrow after school. When I'm home alone."

He got up, unplugged the sphere, placed the globe in the closet, and closed the door.

"Tomorrow," he murmured as his eyes drooped. He just needed some sleep.

Sam went to school that day with a bad case of brain fog. He was irritable, and he wasn't sure why. In class, he felt disconnected. He sat in government class and he was supposed to be taking notes, but he just stared at the whiteboard the entire time. He was aware of Mr. Taylor speaking to the class, but he couldn't focus on his words.

"Earth to Sam. Hello!" Jules called to him.

Sam blinked. "Huh?"

Jules snapped his fingers in front of his nose. "Wake up. Class is over, dude. The bell rang. Space out much?"

"Oh." He looked around the classroom. The other kids were already up, heading out the door.

"What's the matter with you?"

"Nothing." He got up and grabbed his backpack from

the floor, and Jules accidentally bumped into him as he was walking by.

Sam scowled. "Watch where you're going."

Jules turned and scowled back at him. "*You* watch where you're going." Then he bumped him again intentionally as he left the class.

Sam had to step back in order to not fall over. Jules had bumped him on purpose! Sam stormed to his locker to grab his lunch and slammed the metal door closed.

"Hi, Sam." He jumped. Lydia was standing next to him.

He sighed. "Oh, hi, Lydia. Didn't see you there."

"Is everything okay?"

Sam had been adjusting his backpack, but now he looked at her suspiciously. "Yeah, why?"

Her eyes widened, and she took a step back. "Um, you look a little upset, is all."

Sam shrugged. "Just tired today." He wasn't upset. Was *she* okay?

Her lips curved upward. "Yeah, school can get tiring. Um, I was thinking—"

"Yeah, well," he said, interrupting her. "I gotta go." He walked away.

"Oh. Okay . . . bye."

As Sam walked to the bleachers, he wondered why people were suddenly interested in how he was acting or feeling. Normally, people didn't even see him or care to talk to him. Now, when he wanted to be left alone, it was like people were all up in his business.

He sat on a bleacher a row below Raad. "How's it going, Sam?" his friend asked him.

"Fine." But it wasn't going fine. Sitting in the sun, he realized he'd forgotten his hat *and* his sunscreen. He hadn't felt like making a sandwich that morning, so all he had was fruit and it probably wouldn't fill him up. Today was turning out to be a total downer.

"You all right? You look a little tired."

His shoulders went stiff. "I said, *I'm fine.*"

Raad lifted up a hand. "All right. Cool."

Jules butted in from his stance leaning against the side railing. "He was spaced out in government class, too. I think the dream sphere is making him seriously wig out. Think it's time to pass it on to the next person, who can handle it. Me."

"No, it's not making me do anything. I haven't even used it much," Sam said. "I just didn't sleep well—as if it's any of your business. You'll get your turn after the week is over. Now drop it." He turned to Raad. "Every day, he's on my case. *Give me the sphere. Share the sphere.* He hasn't had the sphere yet, and he's already wigging out about it."

Bogart laughed, and Jules didn't like it.

"You're the one wigging out," Jules spat out. "You're probably freaking obsessed with it. You probably use it all day, every day, like the dork that you are."

"I'm not a dork," Sam snapped back. "You're the dork who can't wait his turn."

Bogart snorted. "Look at Sam being all grouchy. Does the sphere make you grouchy? Maybe I should pass on my turn. I like being in a good mood."

Sam's hands clenched into fists. "I am *not* grouchy."

Larry said, "Denial."

Sam stood. "Just shut up! I don't even care if I use the sphere anymore or not. I'm not even going to use it today, either, just to prove you wrong."

"Then hand it over," Jules said.

"It's at home, jerkwad."

"What did you call me?" Jules stepped closer on the bleachers.

"You heard me."

"Let's all calm down," Raad said, always the peacemaker. "Take it easy, Sam. Everyone's just kidding around. Jules, relax, man. I think everyone's a little on edge today."

Sam's eyes began to hurt again. "If I'm on edge, it's because sometimes I don't feel like kidding around with you guys. Okay? Sometimes I don't want to be the target for you to pick on or tell me what's wrong about me. Sometimes I just want to be left alone." He grabbed his lunch bag and stomped down the bleachers to do just that. To be alone. He could see some of the other seniors whispering about him as he stormed off.

"What?" he snapped at a guy staring at him.

The guy just rolled his eyes.

Sam's shoulders were moving up and down with his breaths, and he knew he needed to calm down. He found a small corner against the school building and slid to the ground. He was tired and, yeah, he was grouchy, but he didn't need his friends telling him what he already knew. He took out a banana, peeled it, and ate it. Then he took out his apple and bit into it. He closed his eyes and tried to calm down in order to stop the anxiety clawing at his chest. He wished he had his dad's CD player. But he didn't, so he pictured himself sinking into a dream state with the sphere, where he was always calm and at peace. Where no one could bother him or tell him he was acting the wrong way. Where he was free from anxiety. Where life was safe.

The end of school couldn't have come fast enough. Sam turned off his phone and walked home. He didn't meet the guys in the parking lot. He still felt off, and he wasn't sure what the problem was. He couldn't totally blame the guys. They were the same. Always cracking a joke about someone, often about Sam. But usually Sam brushed it off. Usually Sam avoided confrontation. Today, he couldn't seem to do that. Maybe because of lack of sleep or because he hadn't eaten enough.

He stopped at a mini-mart and looked for something to eat, but everything was processed and loaded up with sugar and chemicals. He eyed an energy drink, hesitated, then walked to the coffee machine instead. He needed a quick energy boost. He bought the coffee and drank it on the way home. He shuddered because it tasted bad, but the caffeine would hopefully snap him out of the brain fog.

He walked by the neighborhood shopping center. Cars drove by on the busy street. A kid rolled next to him on a skateboard. He saw an ad for the Freddy's Mega Pizzaplex at a bus stop. He looked at Glamrock Freddy, Roxanne Wolf, Glamrock Chica, and Montgomery Gator all together looking happy and cheerful. He walked farther, and he saw snow globes in the window for sale. Then the next window had hanging bells. Everything reminded him of the dream sphere.

Moondrop's Dream Sphere.

He had wanted to use the sphere while he was at school. He wanted to use it right now. But he was trying to prove to his friends, to himself, that he could stop whenever he wanted. That he wasn't wigging out about it. That he wasn't obsessed.

Yeah, he was irritable, but if he had another session with the sphere, he knew he'd feel better. The anxiety would be completely gone. The irritation would disappear.

Isn't that all that mattered?

Why should he deprive himself of happiness just because of what Jules thought? He didn't even have to know. Everyone had the right to feel good, to feel happy. Even Sam. And that was what he would do, make himself happy. He finished off the bad coffee, tossed the cup in a garbage can, and then jogged the rest of the way home. He went straight to his room. He was breathing fast, and he licked his dry lips. He dropped his backpack and kicked off his shoes. He opened the closet and put the dream sphere back on his bedside table, where it belonged. He took off his glasses, set his watch to twenty minutes, and pushed the ON button on the dream sphere.

Moondrop spun. The lights flashed, and Sam felt his emotions level out as he slipped into a lucid dream. He was exactly where he was meant to be.

When his alarm went off and he came out of the dream state, he felt relieved and calm. Although, this time, he felt tired, pretty much nearing exhaustion. There was no energized feeling like when he first started using the sphere. He wasn't sure why. *Was he using the dream sphere too much?* he wondered. But then he disregarded that right away.

Everything is just fine.

He remembered to turn on his phone, and a bunch of texts popped up.

His eyes widened. "Oh no."

He'd forgotten that he was supposed to help Raad with his yard work. He squeezed his eyes shut. He hated disappointing people. Especially Raad.

He rubbed his head hard and then quickly texted him:

I am so sorry. I didn't feel well after school and went straight home to rest. I should have texted you and let you know. I can help you tomorrow. Promise.

Raad texted back:

No worries. I got Jules to help me.

Sam's shoulders sagged. Raad was his only good friend. He didn't want to mess things up with him. He got up since his mom would be home soon, but he felt like he could lay around for another hour . . . or two. He went to his bedroom mirror, and he blinked.

He was paler than usual, and he actually had some dark circles under this eyes. His hands were in fists like he was ready to fight someone, and he deliberately unclenched them, rubbing his palms against his thighs. He had a passing thought that maybe it was the dream sphere that was making him exhausted. But then Raad's words came into his mind: *Come on, Sam, what could go wrong with a spinning globe with lights?*

He heard his mom come through the door. He took a breath and pasted a smile on his face, but it felt unnatural so he stopped trying to look happy and went out to meet her.

Conversation at dinner with Mom had been nearly non-existent. Dinner was simple: soup and rice. Sam was tired and if Mom was quiet, she was also tired. Mom got up to put her bowl and spoon in the sink. Sam followed and then turned to go to his room.

"Sam, it's your turn to do the dishes," she told him.

Sam sighed as he turned to face her. "I'm too tired tonight. Can't you do them?"

She lifted an eyebrow. "We made a deal a while ago to take turns, and it's your turn."

"Can't you make an exception?"

"No. I'm tired, too, and I do the dishes when it's my turn whether I'm tired or not. And usually so do you."

He waved a hand. "Fine, I'll do them tomorrow after school."

She sighed. "You know I don't like the kitchen to be a mess."

"That's not my problem," he snapped.

"That's it." Mom crossed her arms. "What is going on with you?"

"What do you mean?"

"I mean, with the bad attitude. It's not like you. Usually, you don't like the dirty dishes to sit because of bacteria buildup." That was true, but at the moment, he didn't really care. "What's really going on, Sam?"

"I don't know what you're talking about."

"Oh, you don't? Look at your shirt!"

"Huh?"

"Look down at your shirt."

Sam looked down at his shirt, and his eyes widened.

"What's wrong with this picture, Sam?" His mom walked toward him and pinched the sleeve of his shirt. "It's wrinkled. You *never* wear wrinkled clothes. You went to school like this?"

"I forgot," he said quietly, and pushed up his glasses.

She stormed past him to his bedroom and raised an arm as if to showcase his room. "Your bed is a mess. Your backpack is thrown on the floor along with your shoes. Your clothes have missed the laundry basket, and you never do that, Sam. *Never.* So I am going to ask you something and I expect an honest answer. Are you doing something that you are not supposed to be doing?"

He stepped back. "What? No, Mom, no. I'm not doing anything bad. I promise."

"Then what's going on? Has something happened at school that I don't know about? Is this about a girl?" She stomped over to the dream sphere. "Is it that thing? What the heck is it doing to you?"

An irrational wave of upset feelings overcame Sam. "No, Mom! Just stop and leave me alone!"

"No. Whatever is going on, I want it to stop! And I want this thing gone, do you understand? Give it back to Raad!"

Sam raised his arms in exasperation. "I will! Just don't worry about it! Stop getting on my case about every little thing!"

"I am your mother, and I will worry about anything I want! Because you are still a child, and it is my job to take care of your well-being. When you understand that, things will go a lot easier!"

His mom stormed out, and Sam went into his room, slamming the door on her and her outrageous accusations.

He threw himself on the bed, tossed off his glasses, and growled into his pillow. He turned his head, and he was face-to-face with Moondrop. "You get me, don't you?"

Even though his mom was home, he set his wrist alarm, pushed on the dream sphere, and stared into the spinning lights.

"Mom, I'm going to stay home from school today."

He'd had strange, uncomfortable dreams, and he'd tossed and turned all night. He didn't understand why he couldn't sleep very well anymore. It must have been the coffee yesterday from the mini-mart. He had stopped drinking soda and coffee for a reason, and now he remembered why.

Mom walked to Sam and felt his head. "What's the matter? You're not feeling good?"

He shrugged his shoulders. "I didn't sleep well last night. I don't have anything major going on at school. I'll email my teachers for today's classwork and make it up."

Mom sighed. "Look, I'm sorry about last night. We were both cranky and took it out on each other. It's been a long week."

He nodded his head. "I'm sorry, too. I've just got a lot on my mind."

"Honey, I know you've been missing Dad a lot right now."

Sam's eyes burned. "It's been . . . hard lately."

"I know, Sam." She blinked quickly a few times. "A day off wouldn't hurt. Just take a break from the weird ball as well. Okay?"

"Sure, Mom. It's video games and bingeing television all day for me."

She smiled. "Now, I know you're not feeling well if you're agreeing with me. When are you giving the ball back to Raad?"

"Soon." Which was true, and it made his chest feel a little tight just thinking about it. He crossed his arms against the awkward feeling.

She kissed his cheek. "Good. Take it easy and rest." A few minutes later, she left for work.

Sam felt that familiar twinge of guilt for lying to his mother, but she just wouldn't understand. The dream sphere was a miracle. Yesterday, he had more lucid dreams with his dad, woven from more memories that he'd forgotten. It felt like he was making up for the years they'd lost. He needed this. He needed his worries, his anxieties, to disappear. Sure, the energizing part of the experience had completely disappeared. But that was okay. He could live with that.

He went straight to the bedside table, where the dream

sphere sat. He hadn't eaten breakfast, but he didn't feel hungry. His stomach wasn't growling so he'd be okay until lunch. This time, after he took his glasses off, he lay down on his bed and got comfortable. He set his watch for twenty minutes.

He turned to his side and gazed at the sphere from his bedside table. He pushed the ON button and the lights flashed across his eyes. Moondrop began to spin, waving his hands.

Sam dropped into the lucid dreaming state rather quickly. He was eight and riding on the motorcycle with his dad. The motor echoed around them. It was the last ride they'd taken together. They were on a road trip, just the two of them. The weather was warm, and the leaves were turning yellow, falling on the road. Sam had felt a calmness that everything was all right. He was safe and protected with his dad.

Dad pulled off to a rest stop with picnic tables and restrooms. Other families were sitting at the other tables. Mom had made them sandwiches and packed snacks and water. Dad set the goods out on the table for them to dig into.

"Sam," Dad started as they sat, eating their lunch, "I'm glad we can have these rides together."

"Me too, Dad."

"You know, as you get older, I want you to experience things that are out of your comfort zone. Don't be afraid to try new things. Go on adventures with your friends. Explore the world. Discover what makes you happy and experience it as much as you can."

Sam nodded with a mouth full of sandwich. "Okay, Dad."

"Above that, I want you to remember to make good and responsible choices. Be a strong young man, and do what's right. When you make a choice in life, there will always be repercussions. Good or bad, depending on the actions you take."

"Uh-huh."

Dad smiled. "You might not understand now, but hopefully you'll remember this conversation when you need to. When you're older, it will be important."

"You'll be there to remind me later. Right?"

Dad chuckled. "I'll remind you, son."

Sam frowned as he relived the memory. He'd done the opposite of what his dad had wanted for him. He'd became a cautious kid that barely tried anything new or adventurous. It had all started when he'd lost his dad from the motorcycle accident. He'd known motorcycles weren't the safest form of transportation but hadn't thought anything bad could happen to him or Dad. But it had. So he'd tried to be careful from there on out. And whenever he felt out of his comfort zone, the anxiety kicked in.

His dad had been his sense of safety. Without him, Sam had built himself a cocoon.

He'd felt that if he made informed and cautious decisions, he'd be safe. But what he hadn't realized was that he was depriving himself of new experiences that could turn out okay. Experiences that could bring him some of that joy he'd lost when Dad had gone. He didn't want to be a disappointment to his dad. He wanted to be a kid that Dad could be proud of. He wanted to feel secure enough to take action and do fun things like go on spontaneous adventures with his friends. To ask a girl to prom, maybe.

He felt he hadn't been the strong young man who made good choices that his dad wanted him to be. Not when he was planning out each and every move in his life with the fear that something could go wrong or something bad could happen to him.

The alarm on his wristwatch sounded.

Beep . . . beep . . .

Sam tried to reach to click off the dream sphere, but it was as if he couldn't lift his arm from his bed.

Hey, he thought. *What's the matter with me?*

The memory shifted. He was back at their old house. He sat at the kitchen table eating cereal before going to school. The television was on in the living room. Dad was saying good-bye before he headed to work.

"See you later, buddy," he told Sam, and ruffled his hair with his hand.

Sam nodded his head. "'Kay."

"Love you, son."

Sam was too enthralled in the TV to answer. In the distance, he heard the motorcycle rumble.

"No," Sam said, trying to pull himself out of the lucid dream. He didn't want to experience this memory again.

The memory altered. Sam watched as his mom picked him up after elementary school to take him to the hospital. She was crying.

"It's your dad, Sam. There's been an accident."

"What happened? Is Dad going to be okay?"

Mom hadn't answered because she hadn't known the answer.

Sam's chest felt tight, and he was suddenly scared. More scared than he'd ever felt before.

"Stop! I don't want to see this!" Sam shook his head, but he couldn't pull himself out of the lucid state. He could barely lift his arm, and it fell back to the bed. It was like his body was too exhausted to move.

Finally, he swung his arm over just enough to turn off the sphere. He sat up and blinked and took a breath. Then his mom burst through his bedroom door.

Sam jumped from his bed. "Mom!"

Mom was disheveled and crying. *But she looked younger, still.* "It's your dad, Sam. There's been an accident."

"What?" Sam's eyes widened. He jerked his head toward the dream sphere. Moondrop was still, and then the little jester was slowly turning again as lights flashed from the sphere.

Sam looked down at the bed and saw himself still in a trance.

"What's going on? What's happening?" He looked back at his mom and was sucked into a memory.

He was back to his younger self, watching his mom pace the floor of the hospital. She kept wiping her fresh tears with a crushed tissue.

The doctor walked into the room. His eyes were tired. "Mrs. Barker, there was nothing more we could do for your husband. I'm sorry for your loss."

Mom had crumpled before his eyes, and Sam had started to cry for his dad.

"*Stop!* Let me wake up for real this time!" With all of his strength, Sam jerked himself up off the bed and slammed his hand down on the dream sphere's button to turn it off.

He was breathing hard. A sheen of sweat had sprouted on his forehead. His hands were clenched into fists, and he was trembling.

He looked at his arms and opened his hands. Was he really awake this time? He rubbed his face. He *felt* awake.

He stood up, but he was weak and off-balance, so he sat back down. He held his head in his hands as it throbbed with an ache in the center of his forehead. Both of his eyes stung. His mouth felt dry. He wasn't sure how long he dreamt, but it had been over the twenty minutes he had set his alarm.

Something was definitely wrong, Sam realized. Since using the dream sphere, his sense of reality was blurring. He'd thought he'd awaken from the dream state when he really hadn't. It was like his control was slipping away.

Not only that, but he was changing.

He was breaking promises and skipping school. He'd been irritable with his friends and with his mom. He was lying to everyone. The urge to use the sphere was always there. When he was at school. When he was lying in bed at night. It was as if he couldn't stop using it. Couldn't stop *thinking* about it.

"This isn't good."

His dad warned him about making responsible choices, and it was time to start.

He had to give the sphere back to Raad. *Today.*

He forced himself up. He walked to his mirror, and then he did a double take. His eyes were bright red in the outer corners. He moved closer to the mirror. "Oh my gosh," he whispered as his pulse fluttered. There was blood in both of his eyes!

He'd read about blood vessels sometimes breaking in the eyes when strained or irritated. He paced back and forth for a moment as his chest tightened. What was he going to do? What would his mom say? Would she blame the sphere?

"It's okay," he murmured. "My eyes will heal. I just have to get the sphere back to Raad. I have to get back to normal, and then I'll figure out something to tell Mom so that she doesn't freak out."

He took a breath and went to the kitchen to make himself a healthy, gluten-free, dairy-free chicken salad with fresh fruit. He wasn't hungry, but he forced himself to eat, and then he showered to wake himself up. He put some drops in his eyes, just in case it would help. He ironed his shirt and pants and got dressed, then grabbed the dream sphere and headed for Raad's house.

It was time to let go of Moondrop's Dream Sphere for good.

Sam knocked on the front door of Raad's house, but no one answered. He heard Brutus's deep bark and he knocked again. Sam tried the handle, and the door opened. *Oh.* Someone had forgotten to lock the door.

Brutus came to the threshold. *"Woof, woof, woof."*

Sam held up a hand. "It's okay, boy, it's just me. It's Sam."

Brutus tilted his large head. He seemed to recognize Sam as he then turned and ran—or waddled—off.

"Raad, you home?" Sam called out as he walked in the house and closed the door. No answer. "Hello? Mrs. and Mr. Dawson? It's just me, Sam. I came by to drop something off for Raad."

It didn't seem like anyone was home. Sam glanced at his watch. The guys had just gotten out of class. He was too early. He took out his phone and dialed Raad.

"Hello?"

"Hey, Raad, I'm at your house. I'm returning the dream sphere."

"Sam, I wondered where you were today. Did I forget to lock the door again?"

"Yeah, looks like."

"My mom's going to freak. That's cool, though. We've gotta do a study session together. All of us. So kick back and wait for us. I know Jules is ready for a turn with the sphere, too."

"You guys are heading here now?"

"Should be there in about . . . twenty-five minutes. Got to drop off a paper to a teacher and then we're coming to my house. We'll see you there, okay?"

"Yeah, sounds good."

Sam clicked off the call and set the sphere on Raad's coffee table. He took a breath and sat on the couch. He started to tap his fingers on his knees as he eyed the sphere.

In the quiet of the house, he thought he heard the dream sphere vibrate. He picked it up, and it felt warm. Or was that just his imagination?

He shook his head and set the sphere back down on the table.

He crossed his arms, then uncrossed them as the lure of the sphere seemed to pull him in against his better judgment. He stared at Moondrop. "Twenty-five minutes. I think that's the perfect time for one *last* experience with you."

His eyes stung, and he blinked. His emotions were a little all over the place. "Just once more. I don't want my last lucid dream with you to be when I lost my dad." Then he gently rubbed his eyes underneath his glasses. "I want it to be good. Actually, I want it to be the best one ever."

He stared at Moondrop as if the plastic figurine inside the globe could actually hear his request. Then Sam rolled his eyes. "You can't really hear me, though. Right?"

He didn't set his watch. Raad and the guys would be there soon to bring him out of the dream state.

He took off his glasses and set them on the table, then lay down on the couch. He switched on the dream sphere and gazed into the bright, spinning lights. He started to think about school and remembered what his dad had said . . .

You know, as you get older, I want you to experience things that are out of your comfort zone. Don't be afraid to try new things.

Within the lucid dream, Sam found himself at the high school. There was a sign hanging in the hallway about prom coming up. He was with Raad, and they spotted Lydia standing at her locker.

Raad patted his shoulder. "Go for it, Sam. Ask her to prom. She's a nice girl."

"Yeah, she's really nice." Sam shook his head. "I don't know if I can do it, though."

"You can. Believe in yourself."

"But what if she says no?"

Raad shrugged in his casual way. "Then she says no. No big deal. But what if she says *yes*? You'll never know until you try."

Sam scratched his head.

"What's the matter?" Raad asked him.

"I feel like there's something weird going on, like, I'm missing something. I feel a little nervous. I usually don't feel nervous here."

"What? Like you forgot your backpack or your phone?"

"No. My backpack is in my locker, and I have my phone in my pocket."

"Must not be important, then. But you know what is? Asking Lydia to the prom."

"Yeah, maybe."

Sam's phone rang. When Sam pulled out his phone and checked the ID. It was his dad. He quickly answered. "Dad? Is that you?"

"Hey, Sam, yeah, it's me. I need you to come straight home after school. I have a surprise dinner planned for your mom."

"Surprise? What do you mean?"

"Your mom sold her first art piece to an art dealer. We're all going out to celebrate. I'm so proud of her. She can't stop dancing around the house."

Sam was confused, and then it dawned on him that in this lucid dream, the dream sphere was giving him the best experience for his last time just as he requested. Moondrop *had* heard him.

His dad was alive in this dream! His family was together, and his mom was selling her artwork. This dream reality was how he wished his life would be.

He grinned. "Okay, Dad! I'll be there. This is great news. I love you."

His dad laughed. "I love you, too, son. See you after school."

Sam clicked off the call, still smiling. He looked at Raad. "I'm going to ask Lydia to the prom," he said. "If she says no, it'll be okay. It's not the end of the world, but at least I'll know I tried."

"Right." Raad smiled back. "Go for it, dude."

Sam confidently walked up to Lydia. She was just shutting her locker door.

"Oh, hey, Sam," she said with a friendly smile.

"Hi, Lydia. Um." He cleared his throat as he felt the beginnings of anxiety claw at him. Then he took a breath and pushed the uncomfortable feelings back. "I was wondering if you'd like to go to prom with me? If you haven't been asked by someone else and if you're planning on going at all . . . I would like to go with you."

Lydia's cheeks turned pink. "Sure, Sam, that would be fun. I would like to go to prom with you, too."

Relief washed over him. "Really? I mean, great! Let's exchange numbers so we can set up our plans."

After he said good-bye, Sam walked back to Raad. "She said yes!" They slapped hands in a high five. "I'm going to the prom with Lydia!" He couldn't believe that he'd had the confidence to ask her and that she'd actually said yes!

"Way to go, bud! Knew you could do it."

Sam jumped up with excitement and he actually jumped really high as if he was floating. Sam couldn't have come up with a better description about how he was feeling.

He felt so good—as if he was floating on air.

Raad waited in the high school parking lot to meet up with the guys. The day was kind of cold, and he should have brought a jacket. Not only that but he felt off today. Uneasy.

"What's up, dude?" Jules asked, and slapped his hand. Bogart and Larry followed behind him.

"Not much, but good news. Sam's got the dream sphere back at the house. We can do a study sesh, and then it's your turn with the sphere this week."

A look of annoyance flickered across Jules's face. "That's cool. But look, my friend Davis works at the Mega Pizzaplex. He says they got in an awesome new arcade game and he says we've got to try it out before the long lines start. Let's head over. It'll be fun."

Bogart said, "I'm in."

Larry said, "Cool."

Raad scratched his chin. "Well, I told Sam . . ."

"Don't worry about Sam," Jules told him. "He didn't even come to school today. He's not going to be up for the Pizzaplex. Sam can miss out this *one* time."

Raad looked at the guys as they all stared at him, then gave a nod. "Okay, let me text him. I'll just let him know we'll meet up with him later." He sent off a quick text to Sam, and the group took off to the Mega Pizzaplex.

"Mega Pizzaplex, here we come!" Bogart announced. "I'm *so* going to conquer this new game!"

Sam's dream continued. He heard his phone sound in the distance with a text, but he ignored it. Now it was testing day and he was taking his SAT. Apparently, there were many answers he didn't know. He looked around and saw other kids biting their pencils, rubbing their heads, having some trouble with the questions like he was.

But this was Sam's dream and he got what he wanted.

His dad's voice drifted into his mind . . .

I want you to remember to make good and responsible choices. Be a strong young man and do what's right.

But that was in real life, Sam reasoned. In his lucid dreams, he could pretty much do all he wanted without repercussions.

"I want to know all the correct answers to the SAT,"

he whispered. Information began to download into Sam's brain. His eyes widened as he suddenly knew all the answers to the questions. He zoomed through the essay questions like a champ. He strolled up to the teacher as everyone stared at him.

"You've completed the entire test?" Mrs. Hooligan asked with an astonished expression.

Sam handed over his test materials. "Yes, I have. Thank you." Then Sam strolled out of the classroom for an early lunch.

He went to his locker, and when he opened the metal door, the Moondrop's Dream Sphere was inside.

Sam jerked in surprise and quickly shut the door. *How is the dream sphere here in my lucid dream?* he wondered. *Why is it in my locker?*

His phone rang. Sam it took out and checked the screen. It was his dad again. *Not now.* He clicked off the call and looked around him. No one was close by, so he opened the locker again. He had an idea.

"You're *my* sphere," he whispered to Moondrop. "No one else's. Let everyone else forget about you. Only I will get to use you."

Moondrop's eyes flashed red.

Sam smiled. He took out his lunch and shut the door, then set off toward the bleachers.

When Sam got there, the guys were talking about who was the strongest in the group.

"It has to be me," Jules said. "I'd say I'm the strongest out of everyone. We all know I'm already the fastest."

"Maybe," Larry said.

"Could be a tie between you and Raad," Bogart suggested.

"Raad doesn't eat more than once a day," Jules said with a laugh.

"I eat when I'm hungry," Raad said with a shrug.

Sam sat next to Raad and leaned in to ask, "Hey, whose turn is it with the sphere?"

Raad frowned at him. "What sphere?"

Sam tried not to smile. "Never mind." Then he shifted toward Jules. "Maybe I'm as strong as you."

Jules laughed long and hard. "Yeah, right! I don't think I've ever heard you tell a joke before, Sam. Good one. You're finally lightening up."

He shrugged. "We're the same height and build. Could be a draw."

"There's *no way*." Jules popped a chip into his mouth and chewed. His stare was intense.

Sam wasn't willing to back down in his own dream. "Well, why don't we test it out?"

"Oooh, this should be good," Bogart said, and adjusted his hat.

"Guys, take it easy. I don't want anyone to get hurt," Raad spoke up.

"It's all good. Right, Sam?" Jules said with a twist of his lips. "So we'll settle this. Let's arm wrestle." Jules tossed his chip bag and sat down on a bleacher, putting his elbow on a taller row, and then opened his hand. "Or are you scared?"

"I'm not scared." Sam got up and sat across from Jules,

placing his elbow down on the bleacher, and grabbed Jules's hand in a tight grip.

Bogart covered their grip with his own, holding them evenly in the center. "Okay, guys. Let's see who's got the real muscle here. Ready—*go!*" Bogart released their hands, and Jules immediately put all his strength against Sam's.

Sam held his ground, and their gripped hands struggled to stay in the middle.

Yes, Jules was strong, but in Sam's dream, Jules wasn't stronger than him. They struggled back and forth for a few more moments. Then Sam adjusted his wrist and pushed with all he had against Jules's arm.

Jules's face turned red, and his arm began to shake.

Sam gritted his teeth and shoved Jules's hand down on the bleacher and released.

"Sam wins! Sam's the strongest!" Bogart shouted. "Holy cow, what do you know?"

"Crazy," Larry said.

Sam grinned and shot his arms up in victory. "*Yes.* I beat you!"

Jules scowled. "I want a rematch! I had a cramp in my arm. Two out of three."

"Jules, come on," Raad said. "Sam won. It's all good."

Then a miracle happened.

Jules shut his eyes, blew out a breath, and just let it go. He looked at Sam and nodded his head. "You're right. It's cool, Sam." He offered his hand for a handshake. "You won fair and square."

Sam took the peace offering, and they shook hands.

But he couldn't stop himself from getting in the last jab. "Glad you accepted that I'm stronger than you."

Jules scowled, and Sam smiled.

A phone rang, again.

Sam mentally pulled back from his lucid dream. *Wait, he thought, is that Raad's house phone ringing?*

Where were Raad and the guys?

Shouldn't they have been at the Dawsons' house by now?

Sam tried to pull himself out of the lucid dream to turn off the dream sphere, but he couldn't move. He could hear a few birds outside Raad's house. Someone started up a lawn mower. He could even hear his own breaths.

He tried to lift his hand from the couch. It wouldn't budge.

"This isn't funny," he said aloud in the dream.

"What's not funny?" dream–Raad asked him with a frown.

"Let me out!" Sam struggled to move his entire body back on Raad's couch, but it was like he was frozen stiff.

Then something that had been bothering Sam finally bubbled up in his brain.

He hadn't plugged in the dream sphere. He'd forgotten. But it had started spinning on its own anyway.

How the heck was the dream sphere working by itself?

"Woof."

Sam's eyes widened. "Brutus!" he yelled out with dread. "Don't come near me!"

"What's the matter with you, dude?" Bogart asked from the bleachers. "Chill out."

"Brutus isn't here," Raad told Sam. "He's at my house. There's nothing to worry about. You're good."

"Wake up!" Sam yelled to himself as he stood up on the bleachers and ran down as fast he could. He started to pinch his arms. He rubbed his face and his head. He even slapped himself, trying to wake himself up. He could feel his heart pound in his chest as he started to blink really fast.

"Please, wake up! I won't use the dream sphere anymore. I know I was using it too much. I wasn't making good and responsible choices. *I know.* Please, just let me wake up!"

He felt a sharp pain on his ear. He slapped a hand there. "Ow!"

He heard the guys call for him from the bleachers, but he ignored him. He needed to wake up from the dream state. He needed to be back in his real-life reality.

A terrible pain erupted on his cheek. "Ahhh!" He grabbed at his face, but he didn't feel anything wrong with his skin. And yet, the tearing pain was there, excruciating and throbbing.

"*Brutus,*" he wheezed out past the fear. He ran all the way to the school bathroom and ran into a kid exiting through the door.

He shoved him aside.

"Watch it, jerk!" the kid yelled.

Sam crashed through the door feeling unbearable

pain in his neck, on his arms, and fingers. He ran to the mirror.

For a moment, relief washed over him as he looked at his face. He looked fine. He looked like himself. His cheeks were red from excursion. Sweat was beaded on his forehead. His eyes were wide.

"I'm good. I'm all right."

Then he saw Moondrop, wearing his star cap, step into the reflection of the mirror from behind him. "What? How? What are you doing here?"

Before Sam could turn to look at the jester, he felt flesh being torn from his jaw. He could hear the echoes of growling and the chomping of Brutus on his face.

"Let me wake up, please!"

Sam screamed as he felt his nose rip off. His lips were being pulled and shredded. His teeth were gnawed on and scraped. He felt warm blood drip down his face and neck. Panic and despair crashed over him like a wave.

Shaking, Sam gripped the sink harder as Brutus ate his face off back in reality.

But as he stared into the mirror, nothing was visibly wrong.

Sam screamed one name: "Brutuuuuuuuuusssssss!"

In the mirror, Moondrop had a smile on his face, half of it hidden in the shadows. The jester waved, the bell on his wrists chimed, and then Sam went very still. He let go of the sink and stood up straight. The terror disappeared. He felt completely calm and at peace. He turned and smiled at Moondrop.

"Everything's fine," Sam said with wide eyes.

Moondrop turned to walk out the door. Sam followed Moondrop to see what new adventure they would create together.

Meanwhile, on Raad's coffee table, Moondrop continued to turn gleefully in a circle, waving his hands, and then slowly stopped.

PRESSURE

UCA JOLTED AND STUTTER-STEPPED FORWARD. HE THREW OUT A HAND TO BRACE HIMSELF FROM THE -SHOVE AGAINST THE NEAREST WALL. HE GROUND HIS EETH AND TURNED TO GLARE AT HIS FRIEND. "CUT IT OUT, NOLAN!"

Nolan laughed and jumped on Luca, wrapping Luca in a playful headlock and dragging him to the red-carpeted floor. Luca easily flipped Nolan off and bounced back to his feet.

"What's up with you today, dude?" Luca asked the muscular, shaggy blond who kept trying to roughhouse with Luca like they were little kids instead of high school seniors. "You drink too much coffee this morning?"

"No such thing." Nolan grinned up at Luca and extended a hand.

Luca shook his head and took the hand. He pulled Nolan upright. Nolan grinned even wider and pulled Luca into a half hug.

Luca gave into the hug, but he wanted to shove the big oaf away. *Friend* was a word he wasn't sure applied to

Nolan anymore. Yeah, he and Nolan and Asher had been hanging out together for a long time, but lately, Luca wasn't sure why he spent time with his two so-called buddies.

Well, actually, Asher wasn't the problem. It was Nolan.

Ever since Nolan had started dating Maddy, he'd been acting like they were a royal couple. Which wasn't so hard when Maddy, Luca's longtime friend, had been crowned homecoming queen this year. Now Luca felt increasingly like he and Asher were the king and queen's subjects. And he didn't like that feeling.

"Should I be jealous?" Maddy asked, possessively putting her arm around Nolan's waist. She winked at Luca and wiggled her eyebrows at him.

He sighed and turned away when Nolan leaned down and kissed his dark-haired—and distractingly pretty—girlfriend. Luca tried to ignore the pressure in his chest.

Maddy's jealousy was pretend; Luca's wasn't. Luca had been in love with Maddy long before Nolan had made his move on her. And Nolan had known how Luca felt.

"You snooze, you lose," Nolan had said when Luca had suggested that asking out the girl your friend was crazy about wasn't particularly cool.

"Come on, you guys," Asher said. "Stop messing around. Check out all these costumes. Let's pick a scenario so we can decide who we want to be."

Luca pulled his gaze away from the still-smooching couple. He turned to Asher, who stood with his arms crossed. He was tapping his foot in dramatic impatience.

Luca suppressed a smile. Asher, six feet two inches tall and wiry, had gotten into theater at the start of their senior year. With thick brown hair and deep brown eyes, Asher was good-looking enough to be a leading man, and he immediately landed choice roles when he auditioned. He'd gotten so into theater that he'd announced he no longer wanted to go to law school and follow in his attorney father's footsteps. This had previously been his goal for as long as Luca had known him. When they'd been little, Asher had always wanted to play "courtroom." Maddy, of course, had always been the judge. Asher was the defense attorney—because that's what his dad was—and Luca played the opposing lawyer. They argued negligence cases (Asher might not have known what the word meant, but he loved it because his dad used it all the time). Luca could still remember some of the trials: the case of the spilled grape juice, the case of the overturned wagon (resulting in a skinned knee), and the case of the stolen toy train. Luca had always lost these cases; Maddy thought Asher should win because Asher was the one who wanted to be a lawyer and Luca was just playing along to be nice.

But Asher didn't want to be a lawyer anymore. "I'm going to be an actor," Asher had proclaimed the week before.

Nolan had laughed at Asher's ambition. "You and everyone else who gets a part in the school play," Nolan had teased.

Luca hadn't made fun of Asher's grand goal. Luca's own ambitions were pretty lofty, too. He already had received an athletic scholarship to a good university. He planned to play ball for four years and study phys ed. He was going to do well in college and then pursue a master's degree in sports science. Then he was going to work his way into a university football-coaching position. Ultimately, he wanted to coach in the NFL. Luca was a good wide receiver; he was fast and agile. He wasn't, however, big or strong; he was five feet ten inches tall and lanky. He knew that sometimes guys his size made it in the pros, but Luca wasn't aggressive enough or confident enough to be one of them. He did, however, think he had the smarts to coach at that level.

Because he figured every dream should have support behind it, Luca wanted to encourage Asher's new aspiration. "Go for it, Ash," he'd told his friend.

The only problem with Asher's new passion was that his theatrics had starting bleeding into the rest of his life. Luca had noticed Asher's gestures and facial expressions were becoming more and more exaggerated.

Now, for example, Asher rolled his eyes at the oblivious, still-kissing Nolan and Maddy, then looked to the ceiling as if seeking divine intervention to part the two lovebirds. He sighed loudly and wandered away.

Luca remained where he was, but he ignored the couple. He turned to eye several rows of animal costume suits and plainclothes costumes. He had to admit he was impressed by all the choices.

When Nolan had shoved Luca, they'd just entered the Costume Closet, their first stop in the Freddy Fazbear's Mega Pizzaplex Role Play venue, "Urban Legend Role Players Auditorium." The huge room, which looked like an obsessive, crazy-rich person's mega closet, was filled with hanging rods and shelves and cubbyholes. All these were stuffed with animal suits and heads, clothes, shoes, and other accessories. Everything was neatly organized and color coded.

According to Asher, who had read up on the game before they'd arrived to play it, the color codes were associated with the various role-play scenarios offered in the auditorium. Once you chose what story you wanted to play out, you picked the costumes accordingly.

As Luca looked around, several kids and teens darted through the rows of costumes. They chattered excitedly as they examined their choices. Luca spotted a few of his classmates checking out a Golden Freddy costume and he smiled at a group of little girls arguing over who was going to wear a Chica costume. Chica, the yellow chick holding an animated cupcake, appeared to be all three girls' favorite Freddy character.

Beyond the girls, a wall-to-wall mirror reflected the costumes and the excited soon-to-be role players. Luca caught a glimpse of himself and his friends in the glass; he cringed. Not for the first time, he noticed the contrast between them. Luca felt like he was the smallest of all the guys he knew. He might be a football player, but he didn't have the ripped muscles his friends had. He was also behind them in the facial hair department. Nolan and Asher, and most of the guys on the team, had been shaving for a while. Luca barely had enough fuzz on his chin to wave a razor at every week or so. On top of all that, thanks to Luca's perpetually tousled auburn hair—he had a cowlick that made neat styles impossible—he thought he looked more like a thirteen-year-old than a soon-to-be college freshman. And once football season was over, he no longer had helmet hair as an excuse.

Luca shifted his attention back to the costumes. He eyed a security guard uniform. Even though security guards didn't generally fare well in Fazbear Entertainment games, Luca wanted to be a guard. He liked the idea of being the hero.

Luca and his friends had been talking about trying out the Role Play Auditorium ever since the Pizzaplex had opened. The VR venue in the Pizzaplex was great, but being on a real set sounded like way more fun. Luca was a fan of horror movies and thought getting to act in a scary story would be a blast. His group of friends, especially their burgeoning star, Asher, agreed.

Between classes and football practice, today's venture had been hard to schedule, so Luca was just as eager as Asher to get started—even if he had to put up with the Nolan and Maddy Show.

The "Urban Legend Role Players Auditorium" was set up for reenacting many of the rumors and ghost stories that had become associated with the Fazbear Entertainment brand over the years. Luca thought the auditorium was a great marketing ploy. He was pretty sure the stories were more fact than myth or rumor. He'd read about the kids who'd disappeared, and he had no problem imagining their corpses stuffed away in the old Freddy's location, their ghosts finding a way to haunt the animatronics that were supposedly still in the abandoned restaurant. If Fazbear Entertainment couldn't shake the rumors, why not lean into them and make some money off the believers? Believers like him, he had to admit.

Asher waved to get Luca's attention. He pointed at a menu board of stories on a wall near the closet's entrance. "Look at this one," Asher said. "It's called 'Green-Eared Killer.' It's about three teens who break into the Fazbear Frights Haunted House and are stalked by Springtrap; they have to try to get away before he kills them. That sounds way cool."

Maddy and Nolan finally came up for air. Maddy sauntered over to join Asher.

The menu board looked like a scoreboard with a list of the available roleplay games. A slate square was next to each game name. A blank square meant the game was open for players. When you picked a game, you initialed the square to indicate the game had been taken.

"I thought we were going to act out the actual haunting," Luca said.

"*You* wanted to act out the haunting," Maddy said. "That's because you're obsessed with murderous animatronics." She flipped her long, wavy black hair over one bare shoulder. "And murderous animatronics are just stupid."

Luca forced himself to ignore the way Maddy's attention—good or bad—made him feel. *She's taken*, he told himself for the thousandth time. *By your friend. Get over it.*

"They aren't stupid. Where do you think Fazbear Entertainment got the ideas for all their games? You think they just plucked the notion of dangerous animatronics out of the clear blue sky? You think it's a coincidence that nearly all their game scenarios have to do with security guards or trespassers trying to avoid being killed? Look at that." Luca pointed at the menu board. "Most of the stories have to do with trying to survive a night in the security office or trying to stay alive while patrolling the old restaurant or trying to keep a music box going so the ghost doesn't get you." Luca felt himself getting worked up. He was sick of having to defend his interests. "It's genius, actually. Fazbear Entertainment is trying to make light of all the stories. And why's that? Because there's truth to them. They keep coming up with games that have you crawling through vents and slamming doors and hiding inside costumes because they know that their animatronics got out of control and killed people. It's all true."

Nolan stared at Luca with raised eyebrows. "Dude, you sound like Grayson from algebra. If you say the word *cabal* or you pull a tinfoil hat out of your pocket, I might puke."

Luca rolled his eyes. Grayson was a geek who talked

way too much in class and was always going on about evil corporate conspiracies and extraterrestrial mind control. "I'm not a conspiracy theorist. I'm just saying that creating games to make light of a bad reputation is a great way to downplay the 'lies,'" Luca made air quotes, "being told about the company."

"Much ado about nothing," Asher said.

"Exactly." Luca nodded.

"Yeah, well, whatever," Maddy said. "I want to be a damsel in distress. Let's play 'Green-Eared Killer.' I'll be one of the teens." She walked up and put her initials in chalk next to the game on the menu board. "The costume code is dark green." She linked a hand around Nolan's arm. "Come on, studboy, let's go pick our costumes."

Nolan grinned at the nickname Maddy had recently started using for him. He affected a cocky swagger as the couple headed down a row of costumes. Asher and Luca exchanged a "going to gag" look and followed Maddy and Nolan obediently. But Luca wasn't happy about it.

Luca had known Asher and Maddy for most of his life. They lived in the same neighborhood. They'd played together as kids and hung out together in grade school and middle school. During that time, Luca had never thought of Maddy as anything but a friend. Always scruffy, with wild hair and buck teeth, Maddy had been a tomboy, and she was just a pal—nothing more. When they'd gotten to high school, though, Maddy—who was strong and athletic—had decided to try out for cheerleading. She wasn't as conventionally pretty as the other girls then—but her gymnastic ability landed her a spot on the squad. Soon after that, she got braces and the buck teeth turned into a perfect smile. She tamed her hair and started using makeup, and the tomboy vibes disappeared, replaced by a gorgeous teenager. In no time, Maddy was the head cheerleader, and this year, she'd become homecoming queen and class president. And Luca was in love. He'd just never bothered to tell Maddy.

Nolan had transferred into their school toward the end of sophomore year and he'd joined the junior varsity football team. Asher was the team's quarterback, and Luca was its star wide receiver. Nolan was on defense; usually he was the cornerback. One day after tackling Luca in practice, he'd made a reference to a horror movie Luca liked. After practice, they'd met up with Asher and started talking movies; that was the start of him being part of the group.

Recently, Luca had realized that though he and Asher still shared interests besides movies and football— wrestling and baseball and tennis and golf and fishing and camping—scary movies and football were about the only things Nolan had in common with either of them. Nolan—a cutup who never took life seriously—had always been cocky, but he seemed to be growing more arrogant every day. Luca was getting tired of it. And then there was the whole "you stole my soul mate" thing. Luca was convinced that Maddy was the love of his life. He'd just been too dense to know it before she'd turned into a beauty queen.

"Here they are," Maddy said now. She waved a hand toward a row of costumes tagged with green plastic discs.

Asher rushed forward and grabbed a pair of khaki pants and a short-sleeve button-down shirt with a plastic pocket penholder. "I'll be the nerdy kid," he announced. "I'll have to work hard to embody the role, but I can do it."

Luca snorted.

Maddy pulled out a short, cotton floral dress. The dress's fabric was yellow and pink; its hem was frilly. "Oh, this is a perfect distressed-damsel dress." She held it up in front of her.

The dress was too girly to suit Luca's taste; however, he was sure Maddy would look good in it. But Maddy would look good in a paper bag.

Nolan reached out and snagged a pair of faded jeans and a black T-shirt. "I'll be the cool dude," he said.

Luca pulled his gaze from Maddy. He raised an eyebrow at the clothes Nolan held. "How are those any different than what you normally wear?" He looked pointedly at Nolan's jeans and dark gray T-shirt.

Nolan looked down. In mock indignation, he said, "These jeans aren't that faded." He grinned at Luca. "Besides, if there's any fake blood involved in all this, I don't want to ruin my favorite duds."

Luca shook his head. He scanned the row of costumes, then turned to the other side of the row and reached for a security guard costume.

"You can't wear that," Maddy said. She stepped up beside him and put a hand on his arm. Her fingers were warm on his skin. He quickly jerked his arm back.

"Why not?"

Maddy pointed at the red disc. "That's not for the 'Green-Eared Killer' scenario."

"Yeah," Asher said. "Besides, we need a killer. If we're all teens"—he motioned to the clothes he and the others had picked out—"you have to be Springtrap."

"The killer?" Luca shook his head. "No way. I'm not going to be the killer."

Luca's friends lined up together and looked at him. "You got no choice, dude," Nolan said.

"Yeah," Asher agreed. "The scenario is called 'Green-Eared Killer.' There has to be a green-eared killer. That's Springtrap. It's the only choice left. So that's you."

Luca shook his head harder. "That's *not* me, and if that's the only choice, we're going to play a different game."

"Says who?" Nolan asked. "You're not the boss here."

"And *you* are?" Luca shot back at Nolan.

Nolan puffed up his already-massive chest. He closed the distance between him and Luca.

Maddy squeezed between them. "Cut it out, you two. You're not going to fight over a roleplaying game." She gave them both scathing looks. "And besides, everyone knows *I'm* the boss here."

Luca actually couldn't argue with that. But he could work with it. He stepped back.

Locking his own gray eyes (a girl had once called them "platinum magic"—he hadn't asked her for a second date) on Maddy's deep green ones, he said, "Let's play a different game, Mads."

Maddy twisted the corner of her mouth. Then she

smiled at him. She turned to Asher. "Want to take mercy on him and play something else?"

Asher shook his head. Flicking a glance at Luca, he said, "Sorry, Luca. We already officially picked it. And besides"—he turned and looked at the menu board—"the other games have been taken."

Luca followed Asher's gaze. Asher was right. In the few minutes he and his friends had been looking at the costumes, the empty squares next to all the other games had been filled in.

Luca turned to Nolan. "You be Springtrap."

Nolan raised an eyebrow. "Why me? Do I look like a killer?"

Asher made a show of looking Nolan up and down. "Actually, with that crazy hair, yeah, you kind of do."

"You've got killer looks," Maddy told Nolan. She squeezed his prominent bicep.

Luca had to look away and press his lips together. He didn't trust himself to speak.

Nolan leaned toward the row of costumes. He plucked a ratty-looking puke-yellow-green rabbit suit off the rack. Holding it out in front of him, he wrinkled his nose. "Wow, this thing is realistic. It's not only gross-looking; it stinks." He thrust it toward Luca.

Luca backed away. "I am *not* wearing that thing."

"You are if we're going to play the game," Asher said.

Luca looked at Asher. "Why don't *you* be Springtrap?"

Asher affected an "I'm as cute as a bunny" look. "I'm way too good-looking to be stuck inside a rabbit suit."

Luca snorted.

Asher grinned and then he shrugged. "Seriously, I picked my costume first. You could have picked, but you didn't."

Luca thought Asher sounded like a five-year-old, but he didn't say so. He looked back at Nolan. "What's your excuse? You're a sick dude; you usually root for the killers in horror movies. Why not play one?"

Nolan grinned. "I don't want to have to kill my girlfriend."

Luca snorted. "It's *roleplay.*"

"You think even roleplay-stalking my girl is going to get me any more kisses today?" Nolan asked, winking at Maddy.

Maddy bumped shoulders with Nolan. She returned his wink. Then she bunched up her brows and hugged herself. "It would kind of weird me out to kiss a guy who'd killed me . . . even if it was pretend."

"And you think *I* want to kill you?" Luca asked.

"You did when I stole your bike in second grade and crashed it into Mr. Weinberg's rose arbor." Maddy grinned. "Remember how pissed he was?"

For a second, Luca forgot about the Springtrap suit and smiled at the memory of Maddy using his stolen bike to try to catapult over their neighbor's big cement cherub fountain. She'd clipped the cherub's wing and ended up launching herself into the arbor. On impact, she'd bent the wheels of Luca's bike . . . and made a mess of Mr. Weinberg's prized climbing roses.

Luca crossed his arms. "I remember how pissed *I* was."

"Exactly my point," Maddy said. "Channel that

feeling." She grabbed the suit and held it out to Luca. "Put on the freakin' suit."

Luca winced as he stared at the suit's matted greenish fur. The costume really was an abomination. Luca knew it was supposed be a rabbit suit, but it wasn't representative of any rabbit you'd want to pick up and cuddle. Like all the Fazbear Entertainment animal characters, this rabbit was a caricature of an ordinary rabbit, like a rabbit created in an evil scientist's lab. With torn ears and patches of yellow-green fur ripped away, the suit's substructure was exposed in several places. It looked old and rusty . . . or *was* that rust? The reddish splotches could have been something else.

After all, the Springtrap suit had been worn by a killer. At least, that was the story.

"You afraid you're going to get cooties?" Nolan mocked in a singsong voice.

Luca didn't bother responding. Cooties weren't his problem.

No, he didn't relish the idea of getting inside the stinky, rotten-looking costume. The idea of putting its metal lining against his skin gave him the willies—he could almost feel himself regressing from seventeen years old to seven. That, however, wasn't why he abhorred the idea of putting on the suit. His problem with being Springtrap didn't lie with the costume; his problem was with who Springtrap *was*.

According to Fazbear lore, Springtrap was the alter ego—the evil persona—of William Afton, the man who had kidnapped and killed little kids at a Freddy Fazbear's

Pizzeria. The real Afton had apparently gotten trapped in a rabbit suit and had eventually died—sort of—inside of it. In the most nightmarish rumors associated with Freddy's, Afton's corpse had come back to life somehow, and in doing so, he'd turned into Springtrap. Fazbear Entertainment made light of this "fable," as they called it. This was why they'd made the character part of the game.

As Luca gazed at the suit now, he was pretty sure he was right in thinking that the fables weren't exactly fables. He had no trouble imagining this suit animated by a real killer.

Maddy lost her patience and shoved the Springtrap suit against Luca's chest. "Take it," she commanded. She pointed to the end of the row of costumes where a neon DRESSING ROOMS sign glowed red above a small arched doorway. "Go put it on."

Without understanding why, Luca grasped the suit when Maddy let go of it. But he almost immediately dropped it.

The suit's fur felt crusty. It was scummy, too, like it was covered with some kind of invisible slime.

Luca managed to hang on to the suit, but that didn't mean he was going to put it on. He looked at his friends. "Why don't we all play teens and we'll just pretend Springtrap is after us?"

"Oh, give me a break." Asher heaved a big sigh. "What would be the point of that?" He stepped forward and poked Luca in the chest. "I thought you wanted to do this. You were as into it as we were when we first talked about it. What's *wrong* with you?"

Luca frowned at Asher. "Nothing's wrong with me. I just don't want to pretend to be a creepy murderer. That's all. I wanted to be the security guard." Luca cringed inwardly. He hoped his friends hadn't heard the whine in his voice. Now he was starting to *sound* like a seven-year-old.

"What? Is pretending to be a killer scary?" Nolan asked. He emphasized the word *scary* in a tone that made it clear he thought Luca was being a coward.

"Yeah," Asher said. "Is it too up close and personal for you?"

Luca made a face. "I don't even know what that means. I just don't want to be the killer, okay? You guys are being jerks."

"They're not being jerks," Maddy growled. "You are! You're acting like a baby. You need to get over yourself."

Asher stepped up beside Maddy. "She's right, Luca. You're being childish. It's just a roleplay game. And that"— he pointed at the suit—"is just dirty fake fur and old metal. It's not going to hurt you. And neither is pretending to be a killer. It's just acting."

Luca looked from Asher to Maddy to Nolan. They were standing almost shoulder to shoulder now, like a phalanx of soldiers commanding him to step in-line and follow orders.

Why couldn't they understand how much he didn't want to do this? Why didn't they get just how wrong it was to pretend to be a murdering maniac?

Well, that was the problem. They believed it was *just* pretend. They weren't thinking about what had really happened. They weren't thinking about the poor, terrified victims.

Luca *was* thinking about the victims.

Not long after Luca and his parents had moved into their neighborhood, about a year before Asher's and Maddy's families had moved in, a four-year-old down the street had disappeared, a little boy named Kenny. Luca's and Kenny's parents were professors at the nearby college and they were all friends, so Luca had played with Kenny. Kenny had been like a little puppy, following Luca everywhere. Luca hadn't minded. He was an only child, and he liked playing big brother to Kenny. He taught Kenny all kinds of things—how to build a castle out of blocks, how to race cars off the porch rails, how to catch frogs down by the stream that ran behind their houses. When Kenny had disappeared, Luca hadn't understood what his parents and Kenny's parents had been talking about when they said he had been kidnapped. He couldn't figure out why Kenny couldn't just come back and play. When Kenny's body was found—in the same creek Luca and Kenny had played in—Luca's parents had tried to explain to him why bad people sometimes hurt good little kids. For months after Kenny had died, Luca had suffered from a recurring nightmare: Every night, he would hear Kenny scream and cry, and he'd try to get to Kenny to save him; every night, he'd get there too late and he'd watch Kenny die. He still sometimes had that horrible dream.

Luca never talked about Kenny. His friends didn't know. Would they relent if he told them now?

Nolan suddenly pushed Luca back against the shelving behind him. "You know what you are, Luca?" Nolan snarled. "You're a coward."

Nolan made as if to push Luca again. Luca backed away, but he locked eyes with his friend. "Don't push me." Luca said the words evenly and quietly, but apparently Nolan got the message. He backed off.

Asher spoke up. "There, see? Just do that, and you'll make a great Springtrap."

Luca shook his head. "I'm not going to be Springtrap," he said. "Hard pass. We need to do something else."

All three of Luca's friends gave him scathing looks. Maddy put her hands on her hips. "You're being silly, Luca. And you're being selfish. Come on. We all agreed to do this. Wear the costume. Please. For me?"

Luca took a deep breath and blew it out. What was the point in trying to explain himself to his friends? They weren't going to get it. And if he told them about Kenny . . . well, they'd probably just make fun of him for having nightmares, for caring so much.

Luca looked at the suit, which he still held. He glanced toward the door leading out of the roleplay auditorium. Beyond the door, the bright lights and happy music and laughter in the rest of the Pizzaplex reached into the room. He could almost feel them call to him, encouraging him not to give in.

He could just leave. Couldn't he?

Yeah, and have it get around the school that the team's star wide receiver had a tantrum over some dumb game?

They were only halfway through the year. The ribbing he'd get wouldn't be pretty.

Luca looked at Maddy. She gave him her sweetest smile.

Luca sighed. "Fine. I'll wear the suit."

Maddy threw up her hands. "Well, *that* was, like, exhausting. You'd have thought we were asking you to kill the Pope or something."

Asher shook his head at Luca. "Drama much?"

Nolan gave Luca a hard look. Then he pointed at the dressing rooms. "Go put it on before you chicken out again."

In the dressing room area, Luca stepped into a cubicle, dragging the rabbit suit behind him like a carcass. He pulled across behind him the small red curtain that draped over the cubicle's opening.

The rabbit suit hung from a wooden hanger, which Luca hooked over a short brass rod extending from the yellow wall. He immediately wiped his hands on his jeans as if he could rub away the stink of everything the suit stood for. Luca stared at the decrepit rabbit costume. Was he really going to do this?

Luca could hear Nolan and Asher bantering in the next couple cubicles as they put on their costumes. "Yeah, right," Luca muttered. "Costumes." All they had to do was put on different street clothes.

"We hear you grousing in there," Nolan called out. "You'd better be putting that suit on. If you're not, I'll come in and do it myself."

"You and what army?" Luca shot back.

Nolan and Asher laughed.

Yeah, yuk it up, jerks, Luca thought. They weren't the ones having to put on an evil costume.

Luca looked at the suit again. Exhaling loudly, he reached for it.

Wearing the Springtrap suit as opposed to the other costumes did have one advantage. Whereas Asher, Nolan, and Maddy had to shed their clothes and put them in a locker before they got dressed up for the game, Luca could put the suit on over his clothes, even over his shoes. Big and baggy, the suit looked like it could fit a guy even bigger than Asher.

The disgusting rabbit suit came in two pieces. One piece was the big, ghoul-eyed, toothy-mouthed, broken-eared head. The other piece was the rest of the rabbit's body; this part of the suit was kind of like a hideous onesie for demented adults. The onesie had hidden closures up the front, so it wasn't hard to get on. All Luca had to do was step into it.

Once Luca shoved his tennis-shoe-clad feet inside the oversize rabbit feet and started to pull the suit upward, he discovered it was designed to expand and contract. Both the fur and the metal skeleton beneath the fur stretched to accommodate his height as he brought it up his legs. When he got the suit to his waist, he only had to contort a little to shrug one and then the other shoulder into the rabbit's torso.

His stomach roiling with reluctance and dread, Luca closed up the suit. He looked at himself in the mirror.

From the neck down, Luca was no longer Luca. He was a moldering rabbit that looked like an escapee from an apocalyptic trash heap.

From the neck up, Luca still looked like Luca . . . sort of. Actually, he wasn't quite himself. His skin, next to the putrid green fur, looked sallow, and his forehead was glistening with sweat. His eyes looked strained, and dark circles had appeared under them. Or was that just the dressing room's dim lighting?

Behind Luca, the curtain swished open. He whirled around.

"Hey!" Luca objected.

Asher and Nolan ignored his protests. They crowded in next to Luca and stared at him. "Sweet!" Nolan said. "Put the head on. I want to see the whole enchilada."

Asher brushed against the torn rabbit fur. He quickly recoiled. "Ew."

"See?" Luca said.

Asher gave Luca a sheepish smile. "I mean, yay. You look great."

"Stuff it," Luca said.

"Just put the head on," Nolan repeated.

Luca felt like an automaton when he lifted the head and pulled it down over his own. When he inhaled, he nearly retched. "It smells like dead fish."

His voice sounded funny from inside the rabbit head— a little muffled and mushy. His vision wasn't quite right, either. He could see, but looking out through the milky-white eyes of the rabbit head gave everything a filmy appearance, as if it was all swathed in gauze.

Luca didn't like this. He didn't like it at all.

Luca started to reach up and take the head off. He'd changed his mind. He couldn't do this.

Before Luca got a grip on the rabbit head, Nolan lifted his hands and tugged the head more firmly into place. He reached around behind the head and snapped something together. "There," he said. "You're all set."

Luca frowned and used his skeletal-looking rabbit hands to try to lift off the rabbit head. The head didn't budge.

"There's a release mechanism in the back," Asher said, craning his neck to examine the suit. "But leave it alone. You look great."

"Yeah," Nolan agreed. "Let's do this."

Luca rotated to look at himself in the mirror again. He couldn't help himself. He had to see the full effect.

As soon as he saw it, he wished he hadn't. He'd gone from being what he'd always thought was reasonably okay-looking to being totally repulsive.

Now that Luca had the rabbit head on, he could see just how vile it was. With exposed yellowish teeth, the rabbit's mouth was a grim maw of desolation. A wire stuck out from the rabbit's jaw and one of the holes in the fur on the rabbit's head exposed more protruding wires. Even more wires extended from beneath the rabbit's dark eye sockets.

Luca lifted his hands and once again tried to pull off the rabbit's head. He shifted his attention to the rabbit's paws. Not so much paws as big fuzzy hands, the coverings over Luca's own hands were missing a lot of fur.

Several of the fingers were exposed metal. Luca's knuckles, beneath that metal, felt entrapped and chafed.

"Stop that!" Asher said. "You're not getting out of this."

Nolan and Asher grabbed Luca, aka Springtrap, by the arms and dragged him out of the dressing room. Luca didn't resist. *I might as well get it over with*, he thought. He'd agreed to it. He'd look like even more of a loser if he backed out now.

Outside the dressing room, a neon sign pointed to a hallway that had multiple doors. Each door had another neon sign above it. The signs labeled the sets for each game.

Luca, Asher, and Nolan paused at the end of the hallway to wait for Maddy. Asher and Nolan started talking smack about how they were going to win the game. Luca ignored them. His attention had been caught by the little girls he'd watched earlier.

The little girls were now playing around outside a game door a few feet away. One of the girls was giggling, adjusting her Chica costume head. The other girl was laughing hysterically because her Freddy head kept falling off. The third girl, dressed as Foxy—the fox character with the eye patch and the metal hook—was lunging this way and that, waving her plastic hook around. She was oblivious to her friends.

She was also oblivious of the Fazbear employee who leaned against the back wall of the Costume Closet. The employee, a lanky thirtysomething guy with a super-short haircut and large ears, was watching the little girls.

The fact that the employee, whose name tag read EARL, was watching the little girls wasn't in and of itself bad. After all, Luca was watching the little girls, too.

The difference between Luca's observations and Earl's staring was that Luca's attention on the girls was benign; he thought the girls' antics were cute. Judging from the expression on Earl's long, narrow face, Earl didn't see cute. His pale blue eyes squinted just slightly, and his mouth stretched into a salacious leer; Earl's interest in the girls was not benign at all. Earl was looking at the girls like they were tasty morsels. His focus was so, well, icky that Luca took a step forward, intending to confront the guy.

Before Luca could take a second step, two little boys raced into the Costume Closet. Screaming in excitement, their feet pounded across the floor. Earl shifted his attention to the boys. But his expression didn't change.

Luca hesitated, wondering if confrontation was the right move. Sure, he could easily handle the guy, but the guy would play dumb, and Luca would look like the aggressor. Luca started scanning the Costume Closet, trying to find another employee—maybe he could report what he'd seen.

He didn't find any other employees. But he did spot Maddy.

"Are you guys ready?" Maddy called out as she skipped toward Luca and his friends.

Luca turned to Maddy. As predicted, Maddy looked amazing in the floral dress. For a second, Luca forgot about Earl. When he remembered, he rotated back to where Earl was lurking.

Earl was gone.

Luca spun in a full circle, searching the area for the skinny guy in the red Fazbear employee shirt. He didn't see Earl anywhere.

"Are you coming?" Maddy tugged on the arm of Luca's rabbit suit.

Luca looked one last time for the unsettling employee. He hesitated. Should he try to find a manager?

Maddy tugged again. "You're not getting out of this. Come on!"

Luca let Maddy drag him down the hall to where Asher and Nolan were already opening the door to the "Green-Eared Killer" set.

Asher grinned. "Let's do this!"

He and Nolan disappeared through the door. Maddy pulled Luca across the threshold behind them.

Each designated area in the roleplay auditorium was a tableau designed to fit a specific game. The "Green-Eared Killer" staging area was a replica of the original Freddy Fazbear's Pizzeria, which also included elements of the Fazbear's Fright Haunted House. From what Luca had read about the Urban Legend Role Players Auditorium before they'd gotten here, all the staging areas were hybrids of multiple locations. Each area was a combined venue packed full of themes from the old stories.

Luca had never been to either the original Freddy's or the Fazbear haunted house, but he'd played the games. He had an idea of what the pizzeria should look like, and this game set was exactly right. He was blown away by its authenticity.

The entrance to the roleplay arena was a crumbling brick archway. Since the Pizzaplex was relatively new, the archway Luca was looking at couldn't have been even a year old, but it looked like a long-forgotten entrance to a place better left not remembered.

Maddy grabbed Nolan's hand and pulled him through the archway. "Look at this," she gushed. "It's totally dope!"

Luca and Asher trailed behind Maddy and Nolan. Their feet made tapping and scuffling sounds on the black-and-white-checkered linoleum floor.

Luca couldn't see the whole place from where they stood, but he figured there would be a dining area with a stage, a backstage area, an arcade, a Pirate's Cove, kitchens, an office, a back hallway, storage rooms, party rooms, and a network of large ventilation ducts running through all of it. All these rooms—at least in the games he'd played—were designed to look old and eerie. They were dimly lit, packed with disturbing Fazbear decor, and populated by knockoffs of the original animatronics.

The actual haunted house and the games based on the house were chock-full of jump scares. Luca assumed this set would include them as well. Although, in the game they were playing, Springtrap—i.e., Luca—was the real jump scare.

"So how does this work?" Maddy asked.

Asher turned in a circle. He spotted a sign next to the archway, and he stepped over to read it. Luca didn't follow him. He was still trying to convince himself he was actually in a disgusting rabbit suit getting ready to chase his friends around a pretend haunted house. Why had this seemed like such a good idea when they'd planned it?

"Okay," Asher said, "according to the instructions here, we"—he indicated himself, Maddy, and Nolan—"are supposed to go down that hallway." He pointed. "There's a little room down there that's like the backstage area of the game. Once we close the door, the door basically becomes what we're going to get through to 'break into' the haunted house. Even though we're breaking in after dark, the venue's attractions are going to somehow get activated, so it's going to be like a haunted house with a chaser. Springtrap's the chaser." Asher pointed at Luca and gave Luca a thumbs-up.

Luca didn't move.

"What's he supposed to do?" Maddy pointed at Luca.

Asher glanced back at the instructions. Then he looked at Luca. "You're supposed to go to the Safe Room. It's a small room at the end of the back hall. You're supposed to go in, close the door, and then wait for the door to open again. Then you come and chase us. Apparently, there's a knife—not a real one, of course—in there someplace. You're supposed to pretend to try to stab us or grab us or whatever."

When Luca didn't respond, Asher said, "Got it?"

Luca nodded. When he did, something rough rubbed at the back of his neck. He reached up to try to adjust the rabbit head. The rubbing stopped, but the skin on his neck felt scratched.

Asher read aloud some more of the instructions. It was

something about how long the game lasted and how you left the game. Luca was only half listening. The scratch on his neck distracted him.

Asher studied the game instructions for a few more seconds. He turned to Nolan and Maddy. "There's some stuff here about ways we can handle Springtrap."

Luca turned toward the instructions. He might as well know the defense's strategy.

Asher blocked his view. "Nuh-uh. No fair. You don't need to know anything else."

"Well, we're on a timer, guys," Maddy said. "Let's do this. Come on." She grabbed Nolan's hand and motioned for Asher to come with them. Asher turned Luca away from the game's instructions. Luca shrugged. What did he care anyway? He just wanted to get this over with.

Asher lifted a fist and offered it to Luca. "Good game, right?" Asher said, just like he did before they took the field at their games.

Luca raised his fist and bumped Asher's. "Good game."

Something poked the underside of Luca's right wrist. He unclenched his hand and dropped it to his side. He watched Asher trot after Maddy and Nolan.

Luca looked around. He shrugged. He knew he'd find the back hallway off the rear of the dining area, so he headed in that direction. As he took his first step, a distant *pop* resounded through the set, and the lights dimmed. Shadows stretched out in front of him.

Luca took a deep breath and a few steps. He winced.

The Springtrap suit was not at all comfortable. Although it had expanded to fit him, it now felt like it was tightening around his body. The metal framework was poking him in a myriad of places. He felt like he was wearing a broken cage.

Luca tried to ignore the unpleasant sensation of metal prodding him through his shirt and his jeans. He crossed the black-and-white tiled floor and headed down a short hall.

Even though the haunted house was dark and gloomy, Luca could see well enough. He marveled at just how chilling the place looked.

The set, like the dilapidated archway, was relatively new. It felt, however, as if Luca was inside a building that had been ravaged by time. Nothing about the place felt fake.

The walls Luca passed as he moved farther into the set looked dirty and moldy, and cobwebs stretched across murky corners and hung limply from barely flickering wall sconces. The mottled walls were "decorated" with old Freddy's posters and decayed parts from Fazbear characters. The parts—animatronic heads, limbs, hands, and feet, along with wires and gears—were caught up in netting or dangling from filthy strings; occasionally, they were pinned to the wall with incongruently gleaming knives. Luca idly wondered if the knives were as fake as the one that he was supposed to use.

Luca didn't linger near any of the walls. He walked as fast as he could in the cumbersome and cramped suit and finally reached the dining area.

The dining area looked like it had been abandoned in the middle of a birthday party. Half-eaten pizzas and half-drunk sodas sat on red-and-white-striped tablecloths next to bright yellow napkins. Freddy Fazbear birthday hats were strewn on the tables and the chairs. The chairs were askew.

Curious, Luca reached out to touch a pizza as he passed a table. Even though he couldn't fully feel it through the suit's decayed-looking rabbit paws, he could tell it was made of rubber. Clever.

From down the hall behind Luca, a crack and thump warned him that his friends were starting their break-in. He picked up his pace so he could get to the Safe Room before they reached him.

At the far side of the dining area, a stage ran the length of the room. Its curtains were pulled partly back, just far enough to reveal statues—at least Luca figured they were statues—of Freddy's original animatronics. Freddy, the bear with the top hat; Chica, the chick wearing an apron and holding a plate with a toothy cupcake; and Bonnie, the purple guitar-playing bunny, clustered near center stage. They were unmoving, but the way their gaze was aimed toward Luca made them look like they might start performing—or worse—any second.

Luca turned away from the stage. He spotted the back hallway, but he was suddenly reluctant to go where he was assigned. Part of the reason he'd wanted to come was to explore, right? Defiant of his friends and the rules, he headed in the opposite direction, toward the arcade area.

Unlike the arcade in the Pizzaplex, which was filled with so many bright lights and emitted so many bleeps and dings and tinny music that the din was overwhelming, this arcade was dark and quiet. All the games looked broken, and they were covered with a hefty layer of dust.

Beyond the grimy arcade, the purple-and-gold-starred curtain to Pirate's Cove was closed, but the hem of the velvet fabric fluttered. Luca stared at the movement, but he shrugged it off. It wasn't like Foxy was *actually* back there.

Maddy's high-pitched giggle echoed through the set, and Luca heard the low rumble of Nolan's voice. Asher said something in response to Nolan, and Maddy laughed again. Luca could hear his friends' footsteps in the main hall. They were getting closer pretty fast. Luca had to move.

Luca headed toward the back hallway and trotted into the inky tunnel. But once he was out of the dining room, Luca hesitated. He couldn't help himself.

This was the infamous hallway, the one the killer used to take the kids to their deaths. Well, actually, it wasn't *the* hallway. This was a reproduction, obviously. But Luca could have sworn it was the real thing. Not only did it look like the narrow, dingy hallway of urban legend infamy, it felt like it could easily be the conduit to a very bad place.

Behind Luca, his friends' footsteps reached the dining area. He started to stride down the hall.

Then his steps faltered. He stopped and listened.

Sibilant sighs wafted through the hallway. They carried with them the sounds of sobbing and childlike pleas.

Luca frowned and shook his head. It was just an audio

track, he reminded himself. This was a fake haunted house.

A chair scraped across the floor in the distance. His friends had reached the dining room.

Luca started trotting down the hall.

As he jogged along, something inside the rabbit suit gouged Luca's forearm. He sucked in his breath.

"What was that?" Maddy asked.

She wasn't really close, but she was closer than Luca should have let her get. He should have been in the Safe Room a long time ago.

Maddy's question, however—although she didn't know it—was a good one. What *was* that gouge that Luca had just felt?

He didn't have time to think about the question for long because the next thing Maddy said was "Oh, look at the animatronics!"

Luca heard Maddy's leather flats tap across the bare floor. Her footsteps reached the base of the stage. "This is so cool!"

Luca listened to Maddy trot up the stairs to the stage just as he reached the doorway to the last room at the end of the hall. Although he could easily hear his friends from where he was, he knew they didn't hear him. They couldn't see him, either. The hall was as dark as any subterranean passageway.

As Luca ducked into the little room, he heard Nolan calling out, "Be careful, babe. This place has surprises."

Luca pulled the door closed.

As soon as the door settled into place, it clicked. Luca

reached out to try to open it. The handle wouldn't turn.
The door was locked.

Although being stuck in a locked room wasn't ideal,
Luca wasn't too worried about it. He figured the game
would unlock the door after a prescribed amount of
time. He turned to look at his surroundings.

But Luca couldn't see anything. The room was
pitch-black.

Luca felt around for a light switch . . . and he quickly
realized that "feeling" anything was a challenge. Inside
the suit, his hands couldn't sense much at all. The only
thing he could do was sweep the paw up and down
over the wall, hoping he might eventually encounter
something.

After a few seconds of groping, Luca was still in complete darkness. Or no . . . not complete. A barely-there
glow reached in around the door's frame. It wasn't much,
but it was enough to ease the tension that had bunched
up Luca's shoulders while he'd groped for a way to turn
on the lights.

Luca tried to see what was in the room. All he
could make out were some squarish shapes that might
have been boxes. He tried not to wonder what was
behind them.

As his eyes further adjusted to the lack of light, Luca
spotted something on the floor. He bent over to see what
it was.

Ah, it was the rubber knife. Or at least he hoped it was
rubber. It looked pretty real.

Luca picked up the knife. He closed his rabbit fist

around the knife's hilt and touched the tip with a rabbit finger. It gave a little. Good. Rubber.

Luca straightened. As he did, the suit pinched him a little tighter around the waist. Something abrasive scraped against his tailbone. Should it be doing this? Could it be—no, he wouldn't let himself think like that. He was too wound up already. This was just a game.

The door made a tiny humming sound. Then, with a suctioning whish, the door opened. Exhaling in relief, Luca grasped his fake knife and hurried out of the room.

Luca quickly headed down the hall. He was ready to pretend-kill his friends so he could finish the game and get out of the rabbit suit.

Once he was several feet from the little room, Luca slowed down. He could hear Maddy's voice in the dining room. She was talking about the animatronics.

Luca padded down the hall. As he went, something poked against his ankle. He rotated his ankle, readjusting his foot's position in the suit. Man, he couldn't wait to get out of this thing.

Luca crept up to the doorway leading into the dining room. He peered past the threshold.

His friends were near the stage. They were still looking at the animatronic statues.

Luca figured now was as good a time as any to get into his role. He lifted his rubber knife, and he prepared to rush into the dining room.

But then the stage lights suddenly burst on. Even more lights flooded the dining room. Eighties rock music blared. A kaleidoscope on the ceiling began to spin, throwing fractals of colored light everywhere.

Although the lights and music in and of themselves weren't scary, the sudden contrast from dim and quiet to bright and loud was disorienting. Maddy ducked into Nolan's arms, and Asher staggered back into a table.

In the harshly colored lights, it was hard to tell, but it looked like Nolan might have gone pale. Good. Served him right. Served them all right.

Asher recovered first. "Whoa," he breathed.

Maddy looked around the room, and her initial fearful expression turned to glee. "Wow! This is so awesome!" She stepped away from Nolan and started dancing. Nolan and Asher laughed and watched her.

Almost as fast as the lights and music had come on, they went off. The previously dim lights went off, too. The entire room was now dark. As the blackness descended, maniacal laughter echoed through the room. The sound of pounding footsteps came from the stage.

Maddy let out a little shriek. Asher gasped.

The footsteps stopped. In the distance, a door slammed.

Luca's heart was racing and he took a long, quiet breath. A few feet from him, his friends were breathing loudly. The haunted house's little series of surprises had gotten to all of them.

Luca should make his move now.

Luca took a second to remind himself of the dining area's layout, and then he strode into the room. He stayed close to the stage, hoping to avoid running into any tables and chairs, and he rushed forward, aiming toward where he could hear Maddy's nervous giggle.

A chair scraped. Nolan swore.

The dim lighting returned. Maddy glanced around and saw Luca, his knife raised. She screamed.

Luca flinched at the sound of Maddy's screech. He reached for her. She screamed again.

Luca actually hadn't intended to scare Maddy when he'd held out his hand. Her first scream had pulled him completely out of character—not that he'd ever really been *in* character to begin with. He'd been reaching to be sure she was okay. When she screamed the second time, though, he realized she was screaming because of him.

"Maddy," he said.

She turned and ran away from the stage, heading in the direction of Pirate's Cove. Luca involuntarily started after her. As he did, the purple-and-gold curtain swished open. Foxy stepped forward and swiped at Maddy with his hook.

Maddy veered out of the way at the last minute. She screamed even louder.

Foxy surprised Luca as much as he did Maddy. Luca jerked back when the fox's hook scythed the air a second time. When Luca jerked, something clamped around his thigh.

"Maddy!" he called out.

Maddy shrieked and ran toward the opposite side of the dining room. Asher and Nolan joined her, and the three disappeared down a long hallway.

Luca glanced at Foxy, and he realized that Foxy wasn't

as real as he'd appeared to be. The fox wasn't an animatronic; it was a statue manipulated by a relatively simple system of ropes and pullies—almost like a three-dimensional pop-up book. It was obviously designed to go through a preset series of moves for a jump scare.

"Guys!" Luca called out.

They must have figured Luca was being Springtrap, but he wasn't. He put a hand to his leg and moaned. Whatever had grabbed his thigh hadn't let go. It felt like a metal trap had glommed onto his leg. It had broken his skin as well. He could feel warmth trickling down over his knee—and the moisture wasn't sweat. He was bleeding. He was sure of it.

From somewhere down the hallway Maddy, Nolan, and Asher had raced into, a door slammed. Loud metallic screeches reverberated into the room. Maddy and the guys tore back into the dining room, but when they spotted Luca limping through the rows of tables, they bolted back toward the lobby. The lights flickered brighter for an instant and then went completely dark again. The sounds of murmuring voices suddenly seemed to come from every wall.

Luca wove his way through the dining area, heading for the front hallway. When he got there, grimacing at the throbbing pain in his leg, the hallway was empty. Where had his friends gone?

They were probably hiding in one of the rooms that opened up along the lobby. Luca started down the hall.

Luca trudged past walls hung with more Freddy's posters, which along here were interspersed with yellowing and curling children's drawings. They crackled as he passed them.

Luca pushed open the door to a storage room. It was stuffed with boxes. He stepped in and looked around. His friends weren't here.

After checking out a janitorial closet and a restroom—both of which were empty, Luca continued on down the hall. When he got to the door leading into the Parts and Service Room, he heard whispering. His friends were hiding behind the door.

Luca reached out, intending to push the door open; before he could, the door swung back. Nolan came charging out, bellowing at the top of his lungs and wielding an animatronic leg.

Luca was barely able to step back in time to avoid getting bashed in the face with the metal leg. "Hey!" The attack surprised him. *He* was supposed to be the killer, wasn't he?

Luca reacted without thinking and grabbed the end of the metal leg. He wrenched it from Nolan's grasp, and Nolan stumbled back. Luca dropped the metal leg and lunged for Nolan.

Nolan spun away from Luca. As he did, Maddy and Asher dashed into the hall. The three linked hands and tore away from Luca, heading toward the end of the hall.

"You can't hide from me," he called out. Again, he wasn't being in character. He meant it literally. If his friends hid, what was the point of the game? Why had they bothered with all this dress-up and charades if he was going to stomp around and they were going to cower in some dark corner?

Luca strode down the hall after his friends. As he did, the rabbit suit shifted, and something gouged him in the ribs. Luca gasped and grabbed his side.

Up ahead, Maddy, Nolan, and Asher ducked into a door on the right side of the hallway. Luca picked up his pace.

He stopped, though, when static spurted from speakers overhead. A whirring sound burst forth, and then the tinkling sound of a little kid's laughter was followed by a child's voice calling out, "Hello?"

What the heck was *that*?

Luca frowned at the speakers as they spit a couple seconds of static and then went silent.

I knew it. In one of the VR games, the security guard used the audio system to play characters' voices to distract Springtrap. What Luca had just heard was one of Balloon Boy's lines. Luca had never liked the perky little animatronic boy holding the BALLOONS sign. He couldn't believe he'd let himself react to the recording of the character's voice.

Luca stepped through the doorway his friends had used, but they were long gone. Luca looked around. He was standing in a duplicate of an old Freddy's security office. The small and dingy room held a scratched wood desk, a credenza, and a dented metal filing cabinet. Clunky monitors, dusty keyboards, and random piles of paper covered the furniture's surfaces. A crooked old black metal fan rotated lazily on the credenza. It creaked as it ran, and the breeze it created rustled the papers.

The office had no windows Luca's friends could have used for an escape. The only other way out was through a vent.

Luca bent over and looked under the credenza. Yep. A vent cover, swinging from one remaining screw, hung loosely away from a duct opening.

Luca crouched down to think.

He shouldn't have done that.

When Luca bent his knees, he heard something snap inside the suit. Something that felt like metal teeth dug into his hip.

Luca let out a yowl of pain. He pressed his hand to the area, and again, he felt something wet and warm run down his leg.

That was enough. This suit was dangerous. Luca wanted out of the game.

Luca stood and strode—well, hobbled—out of the office. He continued on down the hall to its end, where a bright red EXIT sign glowed above what looked like an emergency fire door. He grabbed the handle and pushed down. It didn't move.

Of course. The door was fake.

He'd done it again. He kept forgetting he was inside a game, not a real building.

The game, he vaguely remembered Asher reading, only had one entry/exit point: It was the door beyond the crumbling brick archway. And that door was locked down as soon as the game started. The only way the real exit door would open was if the game time was up or if all four participants pushed the door together. Luca tried to remember what Asher had been reading when Luca was concentrating on the scratch on his neck. Right. The game locked up so the participants being chased couldn't cheat and leave the set. All four participants had to agree to halt the game if they wanted out before time was up.

Okay, so Luca had to find his friends and tell them he wanted out.

But where were they?

Luca cocked his head and listened. Maddy was an avid talker; he figured he'd be able to hear her chattering somewhere.

For several seconds, all Luca heard was silence, but then he heard Maddy's giggle. He shifted to get a sense of where the sound was coming from.

Given how muffled the sound was, he figured his friends were still in the ventilation system. He thought about going in after them, through the open duct under the credenza, but they had a strong head start. No, he was better off trying to predict where they'd come out of the ducts.

He left the office and started down the hallway. As he walked, he thought about where he should go next.

If he were hiding from a stalker, what part of the fake building would he choose?

He wouldn't want to come out in a small, enclosed space. He'd want room to maneuver. He guessed that his friends would head toward the stage or the dining area. Or maybe they'd end up in a party room.

Luca headed back to the dining room. He figured from there, he'd be able to hear his friends and work out where they were going. Then he could be ready to catch them when they left the vents.

Luca tried to pick up his pace so he'd be sure to get in position before his friends got out of the ductwork, but the quick movement triggered another attack from the suit. Something pierced his stomach, and he doubled over, clutching his gut.

"That's it," Luca said. He didn't have to leave the game to get out of the suit. All he had to do was take it off.

Luca reached up and back to try to disconnect the rabbit head from the suit's neck. Asher had said there was a mechanism back there.

But Luca couldn't find anything to activate with his clumsy rabbit paws. He pushed. He prodded. Nothing.

Luca clamped his hands against the side of the rabbit head and tugged on it with all his strength. It was like it had been welded into place.

Okay, so maybe he had to leave the head on. But maybe he could open up the suit and tear it free from his body. He needed to get the metal away from his skin.

Luca attempted to free the hidden fastenings along the front of the suit. As soon as he fiddled with the first fastening, however, Luca heard a click. Right on the heels of the click, he was stabbed in the chest, the solar plexus, and the lower abdomen.

Luca yelled out.

Somewhere in the ductwork, Maddy screamed. His cry must have startled her.

The sound seemed to be coming from a party room near the arcade.

Luca tried to calm himself. He was panting like he'd just run down the hall. He needed to keep it together so he could get to the party room before his friends were out of the ducts. He had to tell them what was going on . . . because Luca was pretty sure he knew what was going on. And if he was right, he was in trouble. Big, big trouble.

Luca started walking again, although walking probably didn't accurately describe the way he was moving. He was more staggering than walking. Pain pulsed in his thigh, his ribs, his hip, and most of his torso. He didn't think the injuries were bad yet, but they'd get worse very quickly if he didn't get out of this suit.

Luca's friends might not have believed the mythology of Freddy's, but Luca did. And part of that mythology was that these old suits could be lethal.

There was a reason Springtrap was called Springtrap.

The original rabbit suit that Afton had supposedly used was a springlock suit. Springlock suits were multiuse suits. They could function as either animatronics or as costumes, depending on which mode was chosen. In costume mode, the metal in the suit acted just like a collar stay or a corset; it provided a sort of lining for the suit. In animatronic mode, the metal would engage, meaning it would spring inward, to provide structure for the animatronic character.

The suits were discontinued not long after they were created because the locking mechanisms were often faulty. They could get triggered by the movement of the costume's occupant. And if they were triggered fully, the metal clamps would shoot out and impale the occupant. Fatally.

Luca was wearing one of the original springlock suits. He'd suspected it since the suit had first poked at him. He'd tried to convince himself that he was wrong. He'd just been feeling the ragged edges of a poorly constructed costume, he'd told himself. Surely, Fazbear Entertainment wouldn't have put a *real* springlock suit in the Costume Closet. At least that's what he'd tried to believe. But he'd known. Deep down, he'd always known.

And now he couldn't delude himself any longer. He had to face the fact that if he wasn't careful—and if he didn't get out of this suit soon—he might be doing more than roleplaying the story of William Afton.

Luca's breath sharpened into staccato gasps as he fully realized his predicament. He knew panicking wouldn't help, but the panic was stronger than his ability to reason.

He hadn't wanted to be Springtrap. He knew the legends, he knew what the suit meant better than any of his friends. Luca's vision darkened as his mind raced.

"Get a grip," he commanded himself. "You don't have time for this." Luca forced himself to slow his breathing. He needed to move quickly—and carefully—to intercept his friends.

In the suit, Luca couldn't square his shoulders—and he was, in fact, afraid to do so. But he tried to do so mentally, pushing the worries to the back of his mind. He stepped carefully toward the wall and used it for support as he inched toward the party room. He moved as gently as possible, afraid to activate any more of the suit.

As he took one step after the other, Luca realized his fear was actually not the real reason for the pace of his breathing. The pain wasn't the cause, either. What was really getting his heart rate going was his anger.

Why had he let his friends talk him into this?

At the double doors to the party room, Luca stopped and listened. A muffled scrape and a tap came from the other side of the door.

Luca slowly pushed the door open and looked into the room.

It was shrouded in pools of darkness. The room's only illumination came from a faint spill of light stretching in from the dining room. Luca waited for his eyes to adjust to the murk, and he tried to ignore the thrumming pain in his leg and torso.

The party room was similar to the dining room in that it held tables covered in red-striped tablecloths. These tables, however, were long banquet-style tables instead of smaller four- or six-seaters. Also like the dining room, this room looked like it had been abandoned mid-party. The tables held the same half-eaten food and drinks, crumpled napkins, and scattered party hats. The party debris here, though, spread beyond the tables. Faded, crinkled streamers littered the floor like straw. Deflated balloons flopped at the end of strings drooping from the ceiling. Dust-covered wrapped presents were piled near the end of one of the tables. Some opened presents lay on empty chairs or were strewn on the floor amid the streamers, but these were freakish—menacing versions of mini animatronics, headless dolls, and cracked handheld games spilled out of the gaping boxes.

Walking flat-footed, as silently as he could, Luca entered the room and started around one of the three extended tables. A shuffling sound coming from the far side of the room stopped him.

When the sound didn't continue, Luca went a few steps farther. A *clunk* and whispers turned him to a statue.

If Luca was going to get his friends to understand the crisis—and it *was* a crisis—he figured he had to wait until they were right in front of him. They wouldn't understand him if he called out. The suit muffled his voice, and between that and his pain, he knew he had to be close for them to understand.

A clinking sound and a metallic *tink* were followed by more whispers. The whispers were louder now. He could hear the conversation.

"It's stuck," Asher whispered.

"Well, whack it," Maddy said.

"I did," Asher said.

"Move over," Nolan said. "This is a man's job."

Maddy giggled.

Luca figured his friends were intent enough on their conversation that they wouldn't notice any sounds he might make, so he started moving again, padding around the end of the tables to get closer to the back wall of the room. There, he could see that the wall held a large grated vent cover. The whispers were coming from behind it.

Maddy's giggle, some rustling, and a sharp inhalation led up to a loud bang. The vent cover vibrated, but it didn't come off the wall.

"You must not be much of a man," Asher said, not bothering to whisper.

"Shh," Maddy scolded. "Be nice. And besides, Luca could be out there."

"You mean Springtrap," Asher corrected.

"Could you two hush and move over?" Nolan asked. "I need room to maneuver here."

"Why don't we try another vent cover?" Maddy asked.

"We've tried two already," Nolan said. "I'm tired of crawling around in here."

Maddy let out a squeak.

"Sorry, babe," Nolan said.

More rustling. A small gasp.

"Okay. There," Nolan said.

Luca sidled to the wall next to the vent cover. He put his back to the wall and waited.

He heard Nolan grunt, and then the vent cover flew off the wall. It arced a few feet into the room and clattered to the floor. Nolan's feet poked out through the vent opening.

"My hero," Maddie whispered.

"Why are you whispering?" Asher asked. "If Springtrap is out there, it's not like he didn't hear that."

Nolan slithered out into the room. Luca considered grabbing Nolan as soon as he was out, but Nolan was the least likely to pay attention to anything Luca said. Asher and Maddy would be more reasonable. Nolan was also the strongest of the three. He wouldn't hesitate to grapple with Luca and shove Luca around; manhandling his friends was Nolan's idea of being funny. Not only was Luca weakened by pain, he was afraid that fighting Nolan would set off more of the suit's locking system.

Luca held his breath. If he remained still, tucked into the wall's shadow, Nolan might not notice him until the others were out of the duct.

Nolan bent over and stuck a hand inside the duct. He made an exasperated sound and yanked his hand back. "Not you, idiot. Ladies first."

"Sorry," Asher said.

More rustling came from inside the vent. Nolan extended his hand again.

"Oops," Maddy said. "Don't look, Asher. This dress is really short."

"Eyes are closed," Asher said.

"They'd better be," Nolan said.

Luca gritted his teeth.

Nolan pulled Maddy out of the vent. She immediately wrapped her arms around him and gave him a long kiss.

"A little help here," Asher said from inside the vent.

Nolan and Maddy ignored him. Asher grumbled and began wriggling out of the vent opening without aid.

Luca hated watching Nolan kiss Maddy, but this kiss served Luca. Nolan's eyes were closed, and Maddy's back was to Luca. They were only a couple feet away.

Luca reached out and grabbed Maddy's arm.

Maddy immediately broke off the kiss. She screamed and tried to wrest herself from Luca's grasp. Luca held on. He started to lean toward her, willing her to listen to what he needed to tell her . . . but as he did, something inside the rabbit head clicked.

Suddenly, metal gripped Luca's skull and his face, piercing through his scalp and the skin around his eyes, his nose, and his mouth. His entire head was encased in what felt like a serrated vise. It felt like hooked prongs now *fastened* the rabbit head to Luca.

The pain was scorching. It was as if a dozen fiery-red pokers were trying to burrow their way into his face and cranium. He screamed.

Even though Maddy was still screeching, she managed to yank her arm free as Luca buckled from this new agony. Nolan pulled her away from Luca. Asher, now out of the vent and on his feet, grabbed Maddy's other hand. The three turned to run from Luca.

"Wait!" Luca tried to call out.

But the word didn't come out right. It couldn't.

Two of the searing metal clasps that had secured themselves to Luca's face curled into his mouth. A third one jabbed through his lips. He could barely move his lips and tongue. "Wait" came out as "aaa." The unintelligible noise he'd managed to make ended in a gurgle because blood was filling his mouth.

Luca coughed and swallowed the blood. He gagged and tried to speak again. All he could do was make another garbled noise that sounded like a ghostly moan.

Nolan, Maddy, and Asher were well away from Luca now, thundering around the end of the tables and heading for the door of the party room. Although they were running, all three were laughing. Maddy's laugh was light and airy. Nolan's was deep and throaty. Asher was chuckling, and he turned back to look at Luca as he followed Maddy and Nolan from the room.

"Way to get into character!" Asher called as the three streaked into the dining room, nearly tripping over one another in their delight.

"Stop!" Luca tried to call out.

The word came out as a throaty "ahhhh."

Luca's friends laughed harder. He could hear their footsteps slap across the dining room floor. He lurched through the party room, knocking into chairs and plowing through the streamers, which seemed to chitter in amusement as he passed. Everyone and everything was laughing. Everyone but Luca.

Luca stumbled out of the party room just as his friends reached the other side of the dining room. They fell against one another in their hilarity as they watched him.

Luca started running toward them, but the molten jabs around his head appeared to be affecting his coordination. He tripped over a chair, and he reeled into a table. Plates and fake pizza went skidding off the tablecloth and onto the floor.

At the same time, a rapid succession of snapping sounds filled the suit. Luca's arms and legs were speared by dozens of sharp projections that drilled through his skin with such depth that he felt like they were going all the way through him. He howled.

Luca's howl stopped his friends in their tracks. They

turned to look back at him; all three of them were open-mouthed.

As a wide receiver who got regularly tackled, Luca was familiar with pain . . . but not pain like this. It felt like every nerve ending in his body was firing an agony message to his brain.

Luca had been exposed to a lot of depraved ways of harming the human body in the movies he'd seen. He'd watched, calmly, all sorts of torture. It had never bothered him; it wasn't real.

But this was. Luca had no trouble believing that what he was feeling was like being flayed alive in a medieval torture chamber. Or maybe it was even worse.

Luca took a teetering step toward his friends. He reached toward them and tried to speak again. "Help me!"

The words came out as "el ee." And behind the words, more gargling sounds burbled from the back of his throat. He tried to clear it, and he made a phlegmy choking sound.

Maddy said loudly, "That's gross!" She grabbed Nolan's hand and pulled him toward a swinging door at the back of the dining room. Asher followed the couple, but in the open doorway, he paused to look toward Luca. He grinned.

"Asher!" Luca called.

Asher's name turned into "A-er." And even that butchered version of Asher's name disappeared into a moan. The pain in Luca's head was becoming even more excruciating.

Asher waved at Luca and disappeared through the swinging door.

Luca pushed himself off the table he'd stumbled into. He shoved aside a chair with his foot.

Looking at the chair, all Luca wanted to do was sink into it. Actually, he wanted to fall to the floor and just wail. No, what he really wanted was to get out of here. And to do that, he had to reach his friends. He had to try to get them to understand what was happening to him.

Luca took a step, groaning at the effort. Then he paused.

Maybe he should just stay where he was. Eventually, his friends would have to come back through here to exit the game. Maybe they'd find him and haul him out with them, thinking he was still playing his role.

There was just one little problem with that idea. The spikelike pieces of metal that had embraced Luca's head like a foul, burr-filled helmet had left multiple small stab wounds. Luca could feel the boreholes through his scalp and the skin on his face. He could feel one in the top of each ear. And now, since the suit's last assault, Luca's entire body was being turned into a sieve. Down both arms and both legs, what felt like relentless screwdrivers were drilling through his skin, facia, and muscles. He was being skewered.

Every wound on Luca's body bled. He could feel that, too. Thick, warm liquid ran along the sides of his face and trickled down his neck. Blood flowed copiously over his arms and legs. How much blood had he already lost?

How much was he losing now? He felt light-headed and woozy.

Luca wasn't sure how much longer the game was going to last. What if he passed out before it was over?

No, he shouldn't wait where he was. He had to go find his friends.

Gathering his strength, Luca managed to get through the dining room, and he made it to the swinging door. When he reached the door, he more fell through it than opened it. He wasn't trying to be quiet about it, anyway. Stealth was no longer in his repertoire.

The swinging doors led to a huge restaurant kitchen. Stainless-steel counters were covered with stacks of pizza boxes. A row of pizza ovens, dark and cold, stood open and empty.

Luca floundered into the room and jolted around the end of a counter, hoping to find his friends crouching behind it. No one was there.

Scanning the kitchen, Luca realized that his vision was even more obscured than it had been when he first put on the suit. Blood had pooled in his eyes. He felt like he was looking through a grisly red veil. He couldn't rub his eyes to clear them because his absurd mangy rabbit paws couldn't reach through the milky orbs of the costume head.

Luca blinked several times to try to clear his eyes. On the third blink, he spotted another swinging door. He wobbled in that direction.

Once again falling through the door, Luca found

himself in the back hallway. Looking toward the dining room, he saw his friends on the other side of the doorway separating the hall from the dining area. They'd stopped, and Asher was messing with something on the wall.

Luca opened his mouth to call out, but before he made a sound, the speakers hissed with static again. Then the spooky voice came through the speakers, "There just isn't room in here for both of us."

Maddy's giggle drowned out the sound of more static before the speakers once again went silent. "That's way too freaky," she said.

Asher laughed.

"Where do you think he is?" Maddy asked.

Asher stepped away from the wall. He looked down the hallway . . . and he saw Luca.

Luca ran as fast as he could. Only about twenty feet separated him from Asher. Crossing that distance quickly shouldn't have been a problem; Luca was known for his speed and agility on the football field.

On the football field, however, Luca wasn't hampered by a rabbit suit that was trying to kill him. Now he wasn't able to get up the speed he needed. Instead, he pitched and rolled down the hall as if he was trying to cross the deck of a ship heaving in a tropical storm.

As Luca moved, he reached out an arm, and he called out, "Ash!" Only a nightmarish soft "a" sound came from his mouth.

Even so, Asher didn't turn and run. Instead, he gazed at Luca with wide eyes and a happy smile. "Incredible, dude! You're nailing it!"

"Come on, you moron," Nolan yelled at Asher. "We're supposed to be trying to get away from him, not admiring his moves."

Asher laughed. "Sorry. It's just that he's doing such a great job."

Luca vaulted toward Asher, attempting to leap onto his friend. If he had to tackle the clueless guy to get his attention, Luca was okay with that.

At this point, Luca wasn't concerned about his movements triggering the suit. The suit was already triggered. The damage was done. Luca's only hope was to get help before the damage was irreparable.

Asher scurried out of Luca's reach at the last minute. Luca fell into the doorjamb. He grabbed at it to stay upright as his friends raced up onto the stage.

"He's kicking some serious stalker butt, don't you think?" Asher said as they ran.

Maddy. "Absolutely! He's like the ultimate monster."

"Shut up, you two," Nolan snapped. "Come on!"

Maddy huffed. "Don't tell me to shut up!"

"Sorry," Nolan said.

Asher laughed. "Dude, you're in trouble." The sound of his words moved away from Luca as Asher ran.

"Shut up, Asher," Nolan said. His voice came to Luca from an even greater distance.

Luca's friends were moving farther way. But he could still hear them.

"Hey!" Asher said. "He told me to shut up, Maddy."

"Oh, he's allowed to do *that*," Maddy said. She laughed.

Asher was about to retort Maddy's words, but Luca couldn't hear them. His friends had gone beyond his hearing range. Their conversation was now a disjointed rumble.

Luca sagged back against the wall. His friends thought he was in character, so much so that the worse things got for him the better they thought he was playing the role. How was he going to convince them that he wasn't playing at anything? How could he let them know he was deadly serious?

This whole thing was supposed to have been a lark. How had it gone so wrong?

Luca pushed off the wall. He knew exactly how it had gone wrong.

Luca paused, eyeing the console that Asher had tinkered with. It looked like a control panel that operated lights and audio. Luca gazed at the panel longingly. If only he could use it to communicate with his friends. But what good would it do? He couldn't speak. The best he could do was gurgle over the loudspeaker. They'd think it was all part of the act. Besides, his rabbit paws couldn't manage the controls.

Luca painstakingly made his way up the short flight of steps to the stage. He stopped and listened.

Maddy's voice, high and spirited, filtered through the curtains at the back of the stage. Luca clomped by the animatronic sculptures and pushed his way through the folds of the heavy fabric behind them.

Past the curtains, Luca found himself in a backstage area stacked with boxes and surrounded by hanging racks holding several Freddy's character costumes. The costumes were similar to the ones in the Costume Closet, but these were fuzzy with dust and smelled of mildew.

Luca brushed past them and aimed toward an open doorway. Beyond that doorway, footsteps tapped in rapid succession before Maddy's giggle faded into the distance.

As Luca quickened his pace, his mind—perhaps seeking a break from the pain—took him back into his memories. His childhood fanned out in his head like a deck of playing cards. He saw snippets of his life for an instant before seeing the next and the next.

His memory cascade stopped on a camping trip he and his parents had taken just before the start of Luca's senior year. The camping trip came so clearly into his thoughts that it activated his senses. He could hear the crackling fire and smell its wood smoke. He could see a clearing in a thick forest of tall fir trees. He could feel the moss beneath where he sat. He could taste the sticky sweetness of the marshmallow he'd just roasted to perfection.

"It's about groupthink, son," Luca's dad said in Luca's inner memory movie.

They'd been talking about why one of Luca's friends, Remy, had recently been arrested for stealing a car. Luca had known him for a long time, and he'd always been a straight-up dude. Luca had asked his dad why Remy had gotten caught up with a group of guys who thought stealing cars for an impromptu drag race was a good idea.

"There's something about the dynamics of a group that can override clear thinking," Luca's dad had said, getting into the subject. "An individual's inner compass can go wildly askew when he or she is part of a group that gets fired up to go in a direction that at any other time would feel completely wrong. People in those situations take actions they normally wouldn't take; they listen to others' ideas instead of their own. Groups tend to dampen our inner voice, the one that tells us what's true for us."

What's true for us. The four words echoed around inside Luca's head as his memory movie went dark. The pain came rushing back, and Luca gasped. His breathing was again coming fast and hard. He could barely take a step without moaning.

Luca made it through the door, and he found himself in a huge storage room. The room was stuffed with stacked boxes. Were they stage dressing, or was the storage area real? Did it matter?

Luca stopped to listen. Were his friends in the room?

For a few seconds, the only thing Luca could hear was the sound of his own ragged breathing. He forced himself to be still and hold his breath. When he did, he heard . . . nothing. He exhaled.

His friends weren't here. There was no way they could be that quiet.

Luca turned to retrace his steps, but his legs gave out. He collapsed to the floor.

In the distance, Luca heard what sounded like the distant buzz of an angry bee. He raised his head and strained to listen. A thud followed the buzz, and then Luca heard what sounded like a trill of laughter.

His friends were so far away. There was no way to reach them. He was just too weak.

Luca dropped his head to the floor. He closed his eyes.

Asher let the door to the "Green-Eared Killer" game fall shut behind him. He started down the hall behind his friends, watching Maddy dance around Nolan. Her eyes were bright, and her smile was wide. "That was great! Wasn't it? Can you believe how awesome Luca was?"

"Not bad," Nolan agreed.

Asher slapped Nolan's back. "Not bad? He was stellar! All we had to do was run around a dark fake restaurant. Luca did all the rest. You're just mad that he was the star and you were a bit player. Kind of like on the field."

Nolan turned and shook his fist at Asher. "Shut up, Ash. You're not funny."

Asher ignored Nolan's threat. He rolled his eyes and waited for the arrogant hulk to turn back around.

"Yeah, I kind of am," Asher said when Nolan slung his arm around Maddy.

Maddy laughed and glanced at Asher over her shoulder. "Yeah, you are."

Asher grinned. Then he stopped and looked back at the door to the game. "Should we go in there and get him? He's probably skulking around in that storage room with no idea the game is over."

"He'll figure it out eventually," Nolan said. "I'm hungry. Let's get changed, then go get a pizza. If Luca's not out of there before we're dressed—and he's as smart as you think he is—he'll assume that's where we went and find us there."

At the word *pizza*, Asher stopped caring about Luca's absence. Asher loved pizza, and he was starving.

Luca's eyes fluttered open. He looked out at soft gray shadows. His mind was mushy, and he felt disembodied, like his consciousness was floating around in the ether, somewhere between awake and asleep. Where was he? He started to sit up.

Luca returned, abruptly and appallingly, to his body. Stinging pulsations flared from his head to his toes. He fell back. He tried to open his mouth to cry out. His mouth wouldn't open.

Everything came back to him.

Luca remembered his situation. He was stuck inside a springlock suit, and it was killing him.

How long had Luca been lying here? Where were his friends? Were they still playing the game? Were they hiding someplace waiting for him to come and stalk them?

Wherever they were, they probably weren't going to come back into this room again. Luca had to move.

Groaning, Luca tried to push off the floor. But he couldn't do it. It felt like his muscles had turned to mincemeat. In a way, he supposed they had. Luca figured the spikelike mechanisms of the suit had dug deep into his muscles, probably very nearly shredding them.

Luca ground his teeth together and commanded himself to rise above the pain and go on in spite of it. He knew how to do that. He did it on the football field all the time.

Luca called on the same determination now. He told his nerve endings to shut up, and he pressed himself up onto his hands and knees. His current situation was his own second and eight at the goal. If he gave up now, he'd lose, and he wouldn't just lose this asinine game. He understood how dire his situation was. If he didn't make his way back to the entrance of this set, he was going to lose his life.

Luca managed to push up onto one knee. From there, gasping at the explosions of misery all over his body, he staggered to his feet.

The second he was upright, Luca more fully processed the severity of his situation. Inside his tennis shoes, his feet were drenched in blood. He could even hear his socks squish when he moved his feet.

Luca tried to look down to see the outside of his suit. Was it saturated with blood?

It was probably a blessing that the rabbit head didn't let him bend his neck far enough to see his legs. He raised an arm, but the lighting was too dim for him to differentiate between blood and the suit's already stained and darkened dirty green fur.

Luca didn't need to see the outside of the suit to know he'd lost way too much blood. Who was he kidding? That wasn't news. He'd known he was starting to bleed out when the suit had locked down on him in the dining room. He'd just been trying to avoid accepting the truth.

The minute Luca had seen the awful Springtrap suit, he'd known that putting it on was wrong. Nothing about the idea of wearing the suit and pretending to be a murderer felt okay to him. Luca didn't even want to *pretend* to be a bad guy. He was Luca, a good guy who liked to do the right thing.

Today, he hadn't done the right thing. And he was paying for it.

Giving himself no more time to stop and process his suffering, Luca got moving. He lurched through the storage room and made his way to the backstage area.

Once again, Luca passed the rows of old costumes. As he went by, a couple of them swayed on the hanging rod. Luca's steps faltered. Had he brushed against the costumes? Why had they moved?

Luca frowned. Why did he have the sudden sensation that he wasn't alone back here? And why did he think that whoever was in here with him was not one of his friends?

Staying as still as his wavering legs would let him, Luca listened hard.

Unfortunately, Luca's rough breathing couldn't be quieted. All he could hear was his own labored inhales and exhales. But wait. There! Just for an instant. Had he heard a hint of movement, just a second or two of the sound of fabric rubbing against fabric?

Before Luca could answer that question, a door slammed in the distance. The sound of small galloping feet followed the bang. In the dining room, out in front of the stage, little kids' voices chattered.

Luca moved forward again.

Parting the curtains at the back of the stage, Luca stepped up behind the frozen Freddy standing at the microphone. Looking past Bonnie's immobile guitar, Luca gazed out at the dining area.

Just inside the entrance to the dining room, three small children huddled together. Their eyes open wide, their faces tense with a combination of anxiety and excitement, the kids gaped at what lay before them.

As quickly as he could, stifling a whimper, Luca ducked behind the leading stage curtain. There was no way he wanted these little kids to see him. Not only was he wearing the horrendous suit, his inability to walk normally or speak at all would terrify the kids, maybe even scar them for life. The last thing they needed to see was a twitching, bleeding version of the already-horrifying Springtrap.

Luca figured he'd wait until the kids went someplace to hide before he made his way to the game's exit and pounded on it until someone came to let him out. Or until he died. Whichever came first.

The kids looked to be maybe seven or eight, Luca thought. Two were girls; one was a boy. All three children were in costumes similar to the ones Maddy, Asher, and Nolan had donned for the game.

Luca was barely lucid; he knew that. He was moving more on autopilot than he was taking conscious action. Some primitive part of his mind was trying to save him. He was pretty sure this adrenaline-driven fight-or-flight mechanism was the only thing that gave his legs the strength to hold him up and propel him forward.

But when Luca saw the kids, his reasoning mind

managed to come back online. They couldn't be here if his game was still going. The game must have ended for his group. That meant Maddy, Asher, and Nolan had left.

Why had they left him in here?

He tried to tackle that question, but it was beyond his mind's current capacity. Besides, it didn't matter. What mattered was that Luca had to find a way out of the game.

"This place is creepy," one of the little girls said. The girl had a cute round face and long blonde hair. She was the one in the flowered dress.

"Duh, Valerie," the boy said. He wore a costume similar to Nolan's. "It's supposed to be creepy."

The other girl, who had black hair that reminded Luca of Maddy's, punched the boy. "Don't be mean!"

In spite of his plight, if Luca could have moved his mouth, he would have smiled. This girl was like a little clone of Maddy.

"So where should we go?" Valerie asked. "If we stand here, he'll find us."

The boy pointed down the main hall. "Let's go that way."

As the kids scampered out of the dining room, Luca started to step out from behind the curtain. He stopped when he heard a skirring sound behind him.

Luca turned.

The pain of his quick rotation filled Luca's eyes with tears. He felt their saltiness sting the gouges on his face as they dripped down his cheeks. He couldn't even brush the tears away. All he could do was grit his teeth and ignore the additional layer of torment.

A tap and a small thump came from backstage. There *was* someone back there.

Luca tried to get to the stage's rear curtain as fast as he could. He was so unsteady, though, he zigzagged instead of going in a straight line. It took several seconds to get to the rear of the stage. There, Luca hesitated. Why was he wasting his time checking out the sounds? It was probably just another kid, one in a Springtrap costume. Luca needed to stick with his original plan. He needed to get to the game's exit.

Luca's head swiveled toward the exit, but he didn't take a step. Something was holding him in place. Was it some kind of mental confusion caused by the blood loss? Or was it something else, something real? Maybe it was instinct. Something—besides his own pain—was putting Luca on edge.

Well, whatever it was, he had to find it.

Luca put a hand out and carefully pushed back the edge of the backstage curtain. He ducked his rabbit head around the thick fabric and surveyed the space filled with boxes and costumes.

Luca saw what he'd been unconsciously perceiving. The thing that had drawn him back here was . . .

Earl.

Standing with his back to Luca, Earl's unmistakable shorn head was about to be concealed inside a cheap, Halloween-costume-like Springtrap rabbit head. The rest of Earl was already covered by an equally cheap-looking, Halloween-costume-like rabbit onesie. Both the head and the body of Earl's suit were designed to look like the one Luca was wearing. Earl's suit, however, was obviously just a costume. It wasn't a real springlock suit like the one killing Luca.

But cheap suit or not, Earl was turning himself into Springtrap. He was dressing up as a killer.

Was it going to be an act?

Or was it for real?

Earl pulled the Springtrap costume head into place. He started to turn around.

Luca jerked his own head back behind the curtain.

What should he do now?

If Luca hadn't been dying . . . and he knew he *was* dying—the idea of getting out of the game was something he was just telling himself so he didn't lie down and give up . . . he would have rushed backstage and tackled the pervert in the rabbit suit. But could he rush fast enough to get to the guy before he ran?

Luca had to try.

Gathering his strength, Luca yanked back the curtain. He charged.

Luca came to an abrupt stop.

Earl was gone.

Luca rushed forward . . . and nearly fell to his knees from the exertion. He stopped and clutched a costume rack. He looked around. Where had the creep gone?

There was no way Earl could have gotten past Luca, so Earl must have gone into the storage room. Luca took a deep breath and went in that direction.

Every step a struggle, every motion torture, Luca

searched for Earl in the storage room. After checking behind just a couple stacks of boxes, Luca was sure Earl wasn't in the room. Luca was making so much noise—he couldn't contain his moans and labored breathing—that Earl could easily have slipped away when he heard Luca coming. But where did Earl go?

While Luca wavered in the doorway trying to focus enough to figure out what to do next, footsteps pattered across the stage.

"Amy, look! These are cool!"

Luca recognized the voice. It was the little boy from the entrance to the dining room.

The kids were back.

"Shh, Adam," a little girl whispered. This was the Maddy clone. So her name was Amy. "Do you want him to find us?"

"How do we even know he's in here?" Valerie asked. "We haven't seen him yet."

"He's in here," Amy said.

Luca moved as quietly as he could past the costumes to get closer to the stage so he could hear the kids. Unfortunately, he was moving so clumsily, he couldn't be quiet. He lost his balance, and his foot came down hard on the floor. He froze at the sound of the *thud*.

Valerie squealed. "Did you hear that?"

"Shh," Amy whispered.

"He's back there," Adam whispered.

"What are we going to do?" Valerie asked.

"We're going to split up and all go in different directions," Amy said.

"I don't want be by myself!" Valerie protested loudly.

"Shh!" Amy sighed loudly. "Fine. You go with Adam. Go hide in one of those rooms off the main hall. I'll head toward the kitchen. He can't get us all at once if we're not together. If he can't get us all, we'll win."

"But—" Valerie began.

"Just go!" Amy commanded.

"Come on," Adam whispered.

A few seconds passed. Then Valerie whispered, "Don't get caught, Amy."

Luca heard scampering footsteps. He heard Amy take a deep breath.

Luca moved as fast as he could out onto the stage. He got there just as Amy pushed through the swinging doors into the kitchen.

And as soon as the doors stopped swinging, Earl raised up in front of the stage. He'd been crouching near the far stage steps.

Luca gasped as Earl trotted toward the swinging doors. How had Earl gotten from the storage area to the dining room without passing Luca?

Blinking to try to clear his vision, Luca tottered down the steps. As soon as he was down them, he saw how Earl had made it to the dining room without being seen. The vent cover near the base of the stage was hanging open. He'd used the ductwork.

Luca turned toward Earl.

But Earl was gone. Again.

Luca started to rush toward the swinging doors. Had

he blacked out for a second and lost time? Had Earl already gone into the kitchen?

A metallic rasp grabbed Luca's attention. He looked toward the sound.

Earl was crawling into another vent opening near the swinging door.

Luca guessed that Earl was going to use the ductwork to sneak up on Amy and grab her. Then he was probably going to drag the girl back into the ducts. No one would find them.

Luca had to stop him.

Queasy and nearly out of his mind with pain, Luca felt the room spin as he attempted to run toward the swinging door. He tried to keep his balance, but his legs buckled under him. He went down.

Fortunately, Luca more slumped to the floor than dropped. He made no sound as he sprawled next to the vent opening Earl had disappeared into.

For a second, Luca lay still. This was the end. He didn't think he could move again.

From beyond the swinging doors, Amy screamed. A patter of footsteps followed the scream. Heavier footsteps followed the patter. Something crashed to the floor. A door thudded. The sound of the footsteps began to recede. Amy started to scream again, but the scream was immediately muffled.

He has her, Luca thought.

Luca was pretty sure Amy had run out of the kitchen and out into the hall. Earl had caught up with her quickly.

He'd probably dragged her into one of the maintenance closets.

Luca pushed up onto his elbows. No way was he going to let that outsider hurt Amy. No way.

Luca bawled in agony as he forced himself to his feet. The sound, though, like every sound he made, was muffled and distorted. He was sure Earl wouldn't have heard him.

Taking a deep breath, refusing to make another sound or even consider the new gush of blood rushing from his thigh, Luca lurched into the hallway.

Something hit the door of the maintenance closet just down from the swinging doors to the kitchen. Amy shrieked.

Luca threw himself forward, willing himself to stay upright. His legs felt as rubbery as the fake knife he'd wielded earlier. His knees buckled twice. Both times, he steeled himself and straightened them again.

He could do this. He could get to Amy before Earl hurt her.

Amy's screams turned into yowls. Several bangs vibrated the maintenance closet door. It was obvious Amy was thrashing to break free of Earl's grasp.

"Let me go!" Amy screamed.

Luca summoned his will and took another step. Calling on the dwindling reserves he had left, Luca propelled himself forward as fast as he could.

He reached the door. Deliberately ignoring the spikes boring into his knuckles and wrist as he moved, Luca grabbed the door handle and wrenched the door open. He thrust himself into the maintenance closet.

The first thing Luca saw when he practically fell into the cramped space stuffed with brooms, mops, and buckets was Amy. Writhing like an enraged squid, Amy churned her arms and legs in a blur of determination. Her eyes squeezed shut in either terror or concentration or both, Amy flailed and fought with everything she had.

No matter what she did, though, Earl hung on to her . . . until he turned and his rabbit head came up. Then Earl's pale eyes, peering through the holes in the rabbit costume head, focused on Luca . . . and they blinked in confusion.

The confusion was just enough to distract Earl. He loosened his grip on Amy enough that she was able to lean forward and bite down hard on Earl's forearm.

Amy must have had a powerful set of teeth because her bite made it all the way through the fur of Earl's Springtrap suit. Earl squawked and dropped her. Amy fell on her butt a few feet from Earl.

Amy cried out when she hit the floor, but she popped back to her feet immediately. Her eyes glazed as if she couldn't even process her surroundings. She darted out of the maintenance closet and pounded toward the dining room.

That's it, Luca thought. *Run, Amy!*

Earl bellowed in frustration and anger, and he started to take off after Amy. Luca, however, wasn't going to let Earl get out of the closet.

Luca jerked himself forward, intending to tackle the man. Instead of tackling Earl, though, Luca fell into him. But that worked, too. Luca's off-balance dive took him and Earl to the floor.

Although Earl tried to throw Luca off, Luca didn't give Earl the chance to gain purchase. Instead, Luca bent himself around Earl and wrapped him in a nelson hold. Earl scrabbled to get free, but even though Luca was dying, his waning strength—and the suit's heavy metal—was greater than what Earl's skinny frame could muster.

Luca had Earl pinned. So he used his advantage.

Luca wrapped his ruined rabbit paws around Earl's neck and squeezed as hard as he could.

Earl tried to buck free of Luca's stranglehold, but Luca's hands were locked into place. It was as if his hands had merged with the metal in the suit. They hooked into Earl's neck and tightened inexorably until Earl's airway was permanently blocked.

Earl's body thrashed against the floor and kicked out at the brooms and mops for what seemed like a lifetime. During that lifetime, Luca's memories spooled out in his mind for one last review. Trailing the scenes from his past, Luca's hopes for the future unfurled in his inner vision. These hopes wouldn't be fulfilled. He wasn't going to achieve anything he'd been so sure he'd do.

Finally, Earl went still.

As soon as Earl stopped moving, Luca let himself give in to the inevitable. His body—everything except his hands, which seemed to be fused to Earl's neck—went limp.

The last thought Luca had before thoughts were beyond him was that his inner compass was working again. His final act had not been someone else's idea. It had been his own.

CLEITHROPHOBIA

KIM LOOKED UP AT THE STAINED-GLASS DOME IN THE CENTER OF THE ROOF OVER FREDDY FAZBEAR'S MEGA PIZZAPLEX. SHE GRINNED AND SPUN IN A CIRCLE, TAKING IN ALL THE MUSIC AND LAUGHTER, THE GLOWING NEON LIGHTS, AND THE CONSTANT MOTION OF THE CROWD AND THE ATTRACTIONS.

A line of cars on Fast Freddy, the Pizzaplex's roller coaster, roared past. Kim gazed eagerly at the coaster's screaming passengers, their hands waving above their heads. She couldn't wait to be one of them. She wanted to go on the roller coaster first.

Kim frowned and looked around. Why were her friends headed away from the coaster's line? She hurried to catch up with them and found them arguing over the Pizzaplex map.

"Let me see it," Alicia demanded, her curls bouncing as she tried to snatch the map from Cole.

Cole easily held the map out of her reach. "We agreed that I was the one in charge of the map."

Eric sneaked up behind Cole and grabbed it. "If you two

are going to keep fighting over this thing, I'll hold on to it."

Kim rolled her eyes. "You know they give those things away, right? We all could have had one."

"I told you," Alicia said, hands on her hips, "that's a waste of paper. It's not good for the environment."

Eric snorted. He threw out his arms to indicate their surroundings. "And *this* is?"

Alicia glanced around. "Well, yeah, that's a good point."

Kim took the map from Eric. He didn't protest and instead looked at her in his usual adoring way.

Kim had met her friends in kindergarten. And Kim had known that Eric had a crush on her since the first day on the playground, and all of the seven years since. He'd never admitted it, but it was obvious. Kim's mom said Eric thought he wasn't good enough for Kim because Kim was a pretty blonde and Eric wasn't particularly good-looking. Kim didn't care about that, but she thought of Eric as a brother, not a potential boyfriend.

Kim opened the map and motioned for her friends to

follow her. Cole looked like he was going to argue, but then he shrugged and hurried up on her right, falling in step beside her.

Kim looked down at the shiny surface of the map. She realized it was upside down, and she turned it over.

Cole poked at the map. "It's like a big donut. See?"

Kim gave Cole a look. "Or maybe like a big *pizza*?"

Cole flushed. "Yeah, that too."

Eric pressed against Kim's left side. He tapped the map, pointing at a cutesy illustration of happy-faced bumper cars. Then he nodded over his shoulder at the real bumper cars, which were careening around a small arena. "We're here," Eric said unnecessarily.

"Ya think?" Cole said.

Kim studied the map. It wasn't an ordinary map with just place names and directions. It was more like a series of cartoon drawings, each depicting a venue in the Pizzaplex and each linked to a drawing of one of the Freddy's animatronic characters. The drawings were prominent; the captions under the drawings were in small print.

Chica, for example, hovered over a drawing of a giant swing that was to the left of the bumper cars. To the left of the swing, a bright yellow arrow pointed at a row of smiley-faced stick figures lining up for roller-coaster cars.

Kim stopped. She pointed behind them. "We need to go back that way."

A couple of older kids bumped into Eric and Alicia. "Watch where you're going!" one of the kids snapped. "You can't just stop in the middle of the walkway!"

Alicia took Kim's arm and got her moving again.

"Come on," Alicia said. "I know you want to go on the roller coaster, but we agreed we'd scope it all out before we chose a ride."

Kim sighed. That was true. This was their first time in the brand-new Pizzaplex, and they'd agreed that checking out all their options first was the best thing to do.

Giving in, Kim let her friends pull her along. As they flowed with the crowd, Kim used her index finger to keep track of what they were seeing.

Her finger traced over a drawing of a costume closet. That was the Urban Legend Role Play Auditorium. The caption under the picture promised "Reality fun at its best."

"There's the entrance to the tubes," Eric said. He pointed at a neon archway just past the Role Play area. The arches opened up to a hallway painted with black-and-white pinwheels that looked like they were spinning.

On the map, the climbing tubes looked like entwined snakes with smiley faces and they were formed into a shape vaguely resembling an extensive castle with seemingly endless loops. This was Freddy's Fortress. Kim shifted her gaze back to the real fortress entrance. She spotted a poster that featured a cute robot under the caption "Meet H.A.P.P.S., the Friendly Mascot of Freddy's Fortress."

Peering at the illustrated map, Kim spotted a tiny rubber-treaded robot with big white hands inside one of the tubes. She smiled.

After the Role Play venue and the climbing tubes, the

map had a drawing of a Tilt-A-Whirl made to look like Chica's cupcake with multiple arms and legs. As Kim and her friends passed it, the real Tilt-A-Whirl zipped around. The whipping motion stirred the air, throwing Kim's long hair across her face. She brushed it back.

A shout coming from her right caught Kim's attention. A crew of Pizzaplex workers were clustered around the AR booth, which stood between the Tilt-A-Whirl and the theater in the middle of the Pizzaplex. Smoke filled the booth's glass enclosure. The crew appeared to be trying to pry the booth open.

Kim looked down at the map. On the map, the AR booth was depicted as a pristine crystal-like globe of "fantasy come to life." She had a feeling no fantasies would be coming to life in there today. She just hoped the AR booth was the only venue with problems.

Alicia tried to drag Kim and the boys into the clothing and souvenir shop as they passed it. Alicia was a shopaholic, and her mom gave her a massive allowance. When they left the Pizzaplex later that day, Eric and Cole would probably be juggling multiple bags filled with every piece of Fazbear clothing available. Alicia thought the boys were pack mules, and they never told her otherwise. No one but Alicia, however, wanted to go shopping now. Eric and Cole took her arms and steered her away from retail heaven. The group continued on.

Just past the shops, the aromas of pizza sauce and cheese wafting from the main dining room enticed all four of them. Eric's stomach rumbled audibly, and Cole complained that he was going to starve if they didn't eat now. Kim was tempted to give in to them because the pizza did smell amazing, but she knew it was a bad idea.

"Do you remember when we went on the Octopus at the county fair after we had burgers?" Kim asked her friends.

The boys went pale, and Alicia laughed. Of course they remembered. Whirling around on a full stomach was never a good idea.

"Um, let's wait until after we do the rides," Eric said.

"Good thinking." Kim smiled as she looked down at the grinning Freddy Fazbear holding a pizza that marked the dining room on the map.

They continued on. Wide-eyed, Kim and her friends passed the carousel. On the map, the carousel looked like a giant sombrero. Adorable caricatures of the Freddy's animatronic characters sat along the wide brim of the hat-like image.

After the carousel, they passed the arcade. Eric started chattering about all the arcade games. Kim looked at the map and saw that Eric had the listed games memorized.

Next to the arcade on the map, a drawing of two crossed laser guns indicated the laser tag arena. Cole pointed at the drawing. "We're definitely going here!"

Finally, Kim saw the roller-coaster line stretched out toward the main walkway and pulled her friends toward it. "Okay, we've been around the whole Pizzaplex." She waved the map. "The only thing left is the theater." She tapped a drawing of a fairy-tale-like castle. She looked at the map again. "Oh, and the little kids' play area underneath it. Can we *please* go on the roller coaster now?"

Eric looked at the map. "Are you sure that's everything?" He tilted his head to look at the underside of the map. "There's an index. Can I see it?"

Kim shrugged and handed Eric the map. He pushed his thick-rimmed glasses up on his nose and ran a finger down the index.

Kim tapped her foot impatiently as she watched more kids lining up for the roller coaster. Exploring was fine, but she was ready to go on a ride!

"Come on, Eric." Kim tried to take back the map.

"Wait a second." Eric clung to the map. His nose wrinkled up in concentration as he flipped the map from one side to the other multiple times.

"What are you doing?" Alicia asked.

Eric held up the map and pointed at the index. "There's something listed on the index that isn't on the map." He put his pudgy finger on one of the index listings.

Kim read over his shoulder. "Ballora's Fitness & Flex."

Eric turned the map over and ran his finger over all the illustrated attractions, showing his friends that Ballora's Fitness & Flex wasn't depicted. "It's not here. See?"

Cole frowned at the map. "He's right, for a change."

Eric elbowed Cole.

Alicia looked around. "Yeah, and we didn't see it when we circled the whole place, either."

Cole shrugged. "Maybe it was planned but wasn't included in the final construction."

"It's weird that they'd put it in the index, though," Eric said.

Kim lost her patience. "Whatever." She grabbed the

map and stuck it in her jeans pocket. "Come on. Let's go on the roller coaster. We'll check out Ballora's later."

This time, no one argued, so Kim led her friends to the end of the line. The map was forgotten as they craned their necks to see the high-tech cars they'd soon be riding.

Five Months Earlier

Grady took one last look at the carousel as he checked the attraction off the to-do list on his clipboard. He felt eyes on him and looked up. A shiny painted wood Foxy on the carousel seemed to be staring at Grady. Grady glared at the pirate fox and quickly slung his canvas service tool kit over his shoulder and turned away. He knew it was silly, but he wasn't a big fan of the animatronic characters. He didn't like that they all had big teeth and they had a way of looking like they were planning something . . . something that wouldn't be good for humans. The truth was Grady didn't love robots in general. Artificial intelligence had never seemed like a good idea to him. He didn't think it was good for robots to have too much control.

Giving Foxy one last "I'm human and you're not, so there" glare, Grady strode out onto the black-and-white tiled floor of the Pizzaplex's main walkway. His footsteps reverberated through the empty entertainment center. Grady started to whistle, but the building's cavernous space twisted the sound into an almost-eerie wail.

That's just too creepy, he thought.

Actually, the whole domed facility kind of got to Grady. Although the Pizzaplex would soon be a place of "fun and frivolity"—at least according to the advertisements—right now it was just vast warehouse crammed full of dormant games and rides. It reminded Grady of an abandoned amusement park or an empty circus tent. He had no trouble imagining ghosts lurking behind all the attractions.

When Grady had first applied to Fazbear Entertainment, answering an ad for a technician, he'd hoped for a nice cushy position at a computer terminal, preferably next to a window—he hated feeling penned in. He'd liked the idea of being a behind-the-scenes programmer. Unfortunately, the job was for a troubleshooter rather than a programmer. It was a hands-on position that required working directly with the Freddy's games, rides, and entertainment venues. That meant that Grady had to be here in the big, silent Pizzaplex day after day, preparing it for its grand opening. And once the Pizzaplex opened, Grady would be one of the maintenance techs. So much for that window with a view.

Someone tapped Grady on the shoulder. He yelped and whirled around.

"Whoa. Sorry, Grady. I didn't mean to scare you."

Grady relaxed when he saw one of his fellow technicians, Ronan, a big, super-fit guy with bushy black hair who looked more suited to be a bouncer than a techie.

Grady shuffled his feet. "You didn't scare me." He'd just been *surprised*. Like the way he'd been surprised to learn that Ronan's favorite pastime was knitting.

The Pizzaplex gave Grady the willies, but he wasn't actually *scared* of anything he'd seen so far. No matter what his imagination conjured, he knew there weren't any ghosts around here.

Besides, the truth was that only one thing really scared Grady. And that one thing actually terrified him.

"Tate asked me to find you," Ronan said. "He's ready to leave."

Grady looked at his watch. "We have ten minutes left on our shift."

Ronan flushed and stuck his massive hands in his pockets. "Yeah, that's what I told Tate, but he said that wasn't enough time to run a full test on anything. He said we should just come back in the morning and do the rest of the safety checks. You know I hate to agree with Tate about anything"—Ronan grinned—"but he kind of has a point."

Grady frowned. "But tomorrow's Saturday. My friends and I planned a whole day of gaming. I've already bought the pretzels and the chips and dip." Grady looked up at Ronan. "I would have invited you, but I knew you'd say no."

Ronan might have looked like he could be an action movie star, but he hated violent video games of all kinds, and therefore wasn't up for Saturday raids. Ronan's rugged face crumpled, making him look like a scolded puppy. "Sorry," he said. "I'm working on a sweater for my cousin."

"No problem," Grady said.

Heavy footsteps thudded toward Grady and Ronan. They both looked toward the laser tag arena, which was tucked into a pool of darkness a hundred feet away.

Tate jogged into view, his long blond hair flying around his head. "What are we waiting for? My girlfriend got two huge steaks and is waiting for me at the lake; we're going to fire up the barbecue. Come on. Let's lock it up and get out of here."

Grady sighed. Tate was such a pain in the butt. Although Tate and Ronan were about Grady's age, Tate seemed to be stuck in high school. When Tate wasn't wearing his Fazbear Entertainment uniform (red shirt and black pants), he was always sporting Hawaiian shirts and knee-length shorts, even in the winter. He belonged on some tropical island, not in a landlocked state a thousand miles from the nearest beach. Tate was weird and annoying and bossy. However, if Grady was being honest, his real reason for disliking Tate was that the guy reminded Grady of someone from his past, someone he preferred to forget.

"I don't want to come back in the morning," Grady told Tate. Grady looked down his clipboard. He only had three attractions left to check. "We only have a few more tests to do," Grady said. "We can probably knock them out in an hour or two, at the most. I'd rather stay late than ruin my Saturday."

Tate made a face. "Well, I wouldn't. I'm ready to hit it. Come on." He punched Grady's shoulder and started to stride away.

Grady didn't move.

Ronan looked from Grady to Tate and back again. His brows furrowed.

Tate realized no one was following and turned back. "Seriously, dudes. Let's go."

"I'm staying," Grady said.

"I'm not," Tate said.

Ronan's brows rumpled even more. "We're not supposed to split up," he said. "And no one is ever supposed to be here alone. That's the protocol. It's starred and highlighted in the employee's manual."

Tate quirked an eyebrow at Ronan. "You read that thing?"

"Didn't you?" Ronan asked.

Tate flipped his fingers dismissively. "I skimmed it."

"That means he looked at the cover," Grady said.

Ronan laughed.

"Ha, ha, ha," Tate mocked. "But I do know about the protocol. It's on that poster in the locker room, too."

"Posters. So he can read," Grady said.

Ronan grinned.

"Whatever," Tate said. "The point is that I'm leaving, and, Ronan, you want to leave. So Grady has to leave."

Ronan looked at Grady. "Come on, Grady." He checked his watch. "It's just two minutes to end of shift now."

Grady shook his head. "I'm not leaving. I'm going to stay and finish up my rounds so I don't have to come back tomorrow."

Tate sighed heavily. He slapped Ronan's arm, then pointed at Grady. "Pick him up, will ya? We'll just carry him out of here. Then we'll lock up, and we can all go home."

Ronan gave Tate a withering look.

Tate blew out air, exasperated. "That's it. I'm out of here." He looked at Ronan. "And since you're my ride, you have to come, too."

Tate turned and strode away. Ronan again looked from Grady to Tate.

"Go ahead, Ronan," Grady said. "I know you have your knitting club get-togethers on Friday evenings. I'll stay and finish my rounds."

"But . . ." Ronan began.

Grady patted Ronan's meaty shoulder. "It's okay. I won't tell anyone I stayed alone. And if anyone finds out, I'll take the blame. Go."

Ronan frowned. "You're sure? I could stay so you aren't alone."

Grady smiled. "You're a good guy, Ronan. But no, seriously. Go. I'll be fine."

Ronan hesitated for another few seconds, and Grady had to shoo him away before he disappeared around the far side of the castle-like theater rising up from the middle of the Pizzaplex.

Grady exhaled and looked up. Stretching for fifty feet or so over the top of the employee area and administration offices, a massive two-way-mirrored expanse looked out over the entire complex. A security station was behind the glass, but it wasn't functional yet.

The exterior of the Pizzaplex had an active security system, but no one was here to man it, and all the cameras were off-line. Fazbear Entertainment was having trouble with the internal computer network. Employee records were being kept in physical files because the system had dumped the data. It was kind of the dark ages, but apparently the programmers were working on it.

A door slammed in the distance. Then the Pizzaplex was silent. Grady turned in a circle and gazed at his dim surroundings.

When the Pizzaplex opened in a few months, it wouldn't be so dim. Nearly every game and ride and attraction in the place was swathed in neon or LED lights. The place would be lit up like a carnival on steroids when it was in full swing. Lights would glow and flash on nearly every available surface.

The Pizzaplex wouldn't be quiet in a few weeks, either. An extensive network of speakers was wired throughout every venue in the place. When the Pizzaplex opened, multiple sources of music would vie with the roars and hums and dings of the rides and games. The shouts and laughter of families and the screams of little kids would fill in the gaps around the rest of the noise. Grady had no trouble imagining what it would be like.

Now, however, the only sound Grady could hear was the huff of his own breath. And the only lights on were the security lights. They cast anemic glows along the walkways and over the various attractions.

During the day, if it was clear outside, the sun shone through the stained glass at the top of the domed ceiling. Today, however, wasn't clear. Plus, it was nearing dusk. Pretty soon, most of the Pizzaplex would be in shadows.

The idea gave Grady the goose bumps. But again, it didn't actually scare him.

As long as he had a way out of wherever he was, Grady

was fine. But if he got locked inside . . . Grady shivered and quickly checked his pockets for the master keys he and every other technician carried. He exhaled when he felt their jagged metal edges and heard their comforting jangle. Okay. He was okay. Grady lifted his clipboard and looked at his list.

Grady had two games left to check in the arcade: Skee-Ball and hoops. After that, he just needed to test Ballora's Fitness & Flex. This shouldn't take too long.

The arched entrance to the arcade was only thirty feet or so from the carousel. Grady hurried down the main aisle of the arcade and reached the long row of Skee-Ball machines. They were painted in bright colors and all watched over by painted wooden cutouts of Freddy's characters. According to Tate, machines number two and number five weren't working properly. Instead of fixing them, Tate had passed on that task to Grady.

For the next several minutes, Grady creatively cursed Tate for his ineptitude. Grady had to check all the sensors and scoring switches before he found the problem in the ball controller. Tate was an idiot.

Grady finished fixing both machines, then returned to the first one to play a game. The techs were supposed to play the games to be sure they didn't have any glitches. It was one of the perks of the job. Unfortunately, Tate tended to concentrate on the playing part, and when there was a problem, he fobbed it off onto Grady or Ronan. Jerk.

Grady played a game of Skee-Ball on both machines.

They worked perfectly. He turned off the Skee-Ball machines and picked up his tool kit.

Taking his kit to the Chica Shots hoops game, Grady performed a diagnostic on it, then turned it on so he could test it. The machine dinged and started blasting tinny '80s rock music. Several rubber balls that looked like round versions of the various Freddy's characters' faces bounced down the slope to the front of the machine.

Grady played a round and managed a score of thirty—he'd only made fifteen baskets! Grady's grandmother would be embarrassed for him. She was a whiz at this game. He and his gran often went to a small arcade not far from his neighborhood. His gran was like a pro basketball player, putting up shot after shot so fast that she regularly scored between 160 and 200. She was a phenom.

Grady shook his head and shut off the machine. His score didn't matter. The machine worked fine.

It was time to move on to the last venue he had to check before he could go home and enjoy his weekend. He grinned as he packed up his kit and slung it over his shoulder. Ronan and Tate could come in on a Saturday and work. Meanwhile, Grady would be home munching on pretzels and playing his favorite game with his online friends.

When Grady turned away from the hoops game, he realized the arcade was even darker than it had been when he entered it. The sun was down. Only the weak security lights created a feeble path of light past the machines. Grady followed it to the main concourse through the

Pizzaplex. There, he paused and checked off Skee-Ball and hoops from his list. He looked at his last task and sighed.

"All right, Ballora," he said, "here I come."

The entrance to Ballora's Fitness & Flex was a relatively (by Fazbear Entertainment standards, anyway) nondescript doorway tucked between the laser tag arena and the lineup area for the roller coaster. The arched doorway, unlike most of the brightly colored, light-wrapped entryways in the Pizzaplex, was made of natural polished wood and had a carved sign above it.

Beyond the doorway, a red-painted hallway sloped downward and led to a long flight of stairs with alternating black and white steps. Ballora's was one of two venues tucked under the main level of the Pizzaplex. The other venue was only partly underground; a portion of Freddy's Fortress, the network of climbing and sliding pipes that snaked throughout the entertainment center, was also belowground. Grady knew this from the planning memos he and the other techs were required to read. Thankfully, he'd never had to check out the pipes. According to the specs he'd read, a maintenance robot, H.A.P.P.S., was designed to keep the pipes safe, but Grady didn't want to be the one to test it out. He didn't want to leave his safety in the hands of newly built robotics.

Grady paused at the base of the stairs. He frowned. Wasn't that what he was going to be doing in Ballora's Fitness & Flex?

A shudder skittered down Grady's spine. He *so* didn't want to do this.

Forcing himself to get moving again, Grady followed the now yellow hallway around a long curve until he reached the big arched entrance to the fitness center. Here, the LED lights and neon were in evidence again . . . although, they weren't on, of course. The fitness center was nothing but a darkened maw.

Grady cleared his throat and stepped through the arch. Using the muted security lights to find the main control panel for the center, he opened the panel and flipped the switches to turn on all the lights in the area.

Shining red neon and yellow LED lights blinked on. White spotlights flooded the space with a nearly blinding glow.

Grady took a deep breath and surveyed the venue he'd most dreaded working on. He tried to ignore the fact that he was shaking.

Ballora's Fitness & Flex was an exercise venue different from anything Grady had seen before. Like a climbing wall, it was a vertical attraction. The starting platform was fifty feet up in the air, reached by a long ladder. An intricate series of serpentine tubes led from the platform to the floor. The tunnels were made of clear plastic, and they tapered from a couple feet wide at the top to what appeared to be barely wide enough for a teenager to squeeze through at the bottom. All of them were visible behind the transparent wall that enclosed them. Grady shivered. It looked like an ant farm.

The idea behind the venue, Grady knew, was to force participants to wriggle and pull themselves through the tight spaces, requiring them to twist and turn and stretch themselves around the curves of the tunnels to get to the bottom. All this physical activity was designed to provide aerobic, strengthening, and flexibility conditioning . . . and, theoretically, a lot of fun. Grady was more than skeptical about the fun.

It was a creative idea, Grady had to admit. But it was still exercise. Grady hated exercise.

When Grady, Ronan, and Tate had first sat down to divvy up the list of attractions that needed to be tested, Grady had taken a hard pass on Ballora's. "My idea of exercise is walking from my gaming chair to my fridge," he'd said. "Does it sound like I'm the right person to test a fitness center?"

Tate had lifted a brow and cocked his head as if conceding the point. But then he'd gestured at Ronan. "I don't think Mr. Universe here could make it through the narrow tunnels."

Ronan had nodded. "Unfortunately, it's designed more for kids and ordinary-size adults."

Grady had pointed at Tate. "What about you?"

Tate tossed up his hands in insincere apology. "Bad knees, I'm afraid. And I'm a lot taller than you are. It makes the most sense for you to do it."

Grady had shaken his head. "I hate small spaces." He realized as soon as he said the words that they'd come out in a whiny voice, as if his five-year-old self had piped up to protest. He cleared his throat.

Tate poked Ronan in the shoulder. "I bet Ronan's not a fan of them either since he doesn't *fit* in them." Tate chuckled.

It had taken every ounce of will Grady had not to launch himself across the table they'd sat at and wrap his hands around Tate's throat. When Grady had faced off with the Tate look-alike from his past, he'd been too young to do anything but cry. Now he was bigger, and he could have throttled Tate . . . if he didn't mind going to jail.

Grady shook his head, bringing himself back to Ballora's Fitness & Flex. His legs suddenly felt shaky. Grady sat down cross-legged on the bright yellow tiled floor and pulled out a candy bar he'd stashed in his tool kit, under the needle-nosed pliers. They weren't supposed to eat on the job. Food was only allowed in the employee breakroom. But to heck with the rules. When Grady got hungry, he needed to eat. And when he got scared . . .

Grady unwrapped the bar and bit into the chocolate and nougat. He immediately felt his anxiety ease. Food had always been his comfort.

It was amazing, Grady thought, *how patterns established in childhood stayed with you into adulthood.* Grady was almost twenty-eight years old, and his daily reactions were nearly all dictated by experiences he had when he was little. The food, for example. And his biggest fear.

Grady choked on his next bite of candy as he looked up at the meandering tunnels in front of him. He felt a trickle of sweat run down his side.

Grady closed his eyes. He tried to calm his breathing.

It had been just one evening of his life. Six hours and thirteen minutes. That was all. Grady did the math in his head. Of the roughly fifteen million minutes he'd been alive, the 373 minutes of his ordeal was just an infinitesimal percentage of the totality of his experience. But the impact of it . . . that was another story.

When Grady was little, his parents had loved to dance. They didn't dance much now. His dad had slipped discs, and his mom had never fully recovered from a broken ankle. But twenty-three years ago, at least three or four times a week, Grady's parents had gone to a dance studio to practice for amateur dance contests. This meant Grady was left with a lot of babysitters.

It wasn't like Grady's parents were bad parents or anything. When she wasn't dancing, his mom stayed home and took care of him. He always had milk and cookies waiting for him when he got home from school, and she usually took him to the park or let him have a playdate before dinner. His dad worked a normal nine-to-five, and he played with Grady during the evenings he and Grady's mom weren't out dancing.

They weren't neglectful. They just weren't that discerning when it came to choosing babysitters. At least not that one night.

Grady's regular babysitter hadn't been available. They'd had to hire a girl they'd never used before. She'd been recommended by a friend, but it turns out the friend wasn't a very attentive mother and didn't really care who was taking care of her kid.

Francis seemed nice enough when she'd arrived that night. She was cute and perky, and she smiled at Grady and asked him about the tower of blocks he was building in front of the fireplace. She told him that they'd play a lot of fun games while his parents were out.

Right after his parents had left, Francis had made him a peanut butter sandwich. Grady had been halfway through his sandwich when the doorbell rang. Grady had heard Francis's delighted giggle when she opened the door. He'd wondered what she was so happy about. He hoped he'd be happy about it, too.

But he wasn't.

When Francis had returned to the living room, she had a teenage boy in tow. The boy, dressed in baggy shorts and a flowery floppy shirt, was tall and skinny, and he had scraggly long blond hair.

Thinking about it now, Grady thought it was uncanny how much Tate resembled the boy who had showed up that night. The boy even had Tate's cocky grin, but when he'd arrived that evening, he hadn't bothered using the grin on Grady. As soon as he spotted Grady, the boy gave Grady a dismissive glance and then grabbed Francis and kissed her. Grady had looked away. He didn't like to watch kissing.

"This is Boone," Francis had told Grady. "Boone, this is Grady."

Boone had ignored Grady and kissed Francis again. When Francis had giggled and half pushed Boone away— she didn't look like she really meant it—Boone had looked down at Grady. "You like hide-and-seek, kid?" Boone had asked.

Grady, working to get peanut butter off the roof of his mouth, nodded eagerly.

"Good," Boone had said. Then, weirdly, Boone had disappeared down the hall.

Grady didn't know much at five years old, but he knew it wasn't nice to wander around someone else's house. He'd once tried to do that when his mom took him with her to visit a friend. When Grady wandered off to explore the unfamiliar surroundings, his mom had called him back. "It's not polite to look around other people's houses without their permission," she'd told him. That was what Boone was doing. Grady could hear Boone opening and closing doors. Grady was going to tell on Boone when his mom got home.

Boone finally returned, and when he did, he held out a hand. He finally smiled at Grady.

Grady jumped up, forgetting all about Boone's bad behavior. Grady was ready to play!

Boone took Grady's hand and led him out of the living room. Grady wasn't sure what was going to happen next because hide-and-seek didn't usually start with hand-holding. But he went along when Boone walked down the hall to the linen closet.

When they got to the closet, Boone opened the closet door. Before Grady could react, Boone shoved Grady under the bottom shelf in the closet. "You hide there," Boone had said.

The area under the bottom shelf wasn't big, and it wasn't empty. His mom kept packages of toilet paper tucked under the shelf. There was barely enough room for Grady to squeeze in next to the puffy rolls.

Grady opened his mouth to ask how Grady could win the game if Boone already knew where he was hiding. He didn't get the words out, though. Boone didn't give him a chance. Boone shut the door, leaving Grady in the tiny, dark space.

"Now," Boone said, his voice muffled by the door, "we can seek some fun times." Boone laughed, and Francis giggled.

Grady had immediately kicked at the door. "Hey," he called. "Let me out!"

Boone's laugh and Francis's giggle answered his cry. Both the laugh and the giggle came from farther away.

Grady called out to them again. When they didn't answer, he tried to reach up in front of the shelf to turn the door-knob. His arm was skinny, but the space between the shelf and the door was even skinnier. Grady started to cry as the edge of the wood shelf scraped at his bare arm. He cried even harder when he realized he couldn't reach high enough to grasp the doorknob.

Grady tried to pull his arm back down, but he couldn't. It was stuck.

That's when Grady started screaming. And that's when the 373 minutes started. (The fact that Grady was able to count to 373 at the age of five was pretty amazing, his parents later told him. At the time, though, he had no idea he was doing something clever . . . and whenever he'd thought about it later, he'd wished he hadn't had to do it.)

Grady knew it was 373 minutes because he'd just learned to tell time the week before, and his parents had given him a big orange watch—the kind with an old-fashioned clock face, not the kind with just numbers—as a reward for how fast he'd learned. The watch had glow-in-the-dark hands so he could see the time at night. Thanks to those hands, Grady could see the minutes going by even in the near darkness of the closet.

After his initial panic, Grady had managed to change his position and pull his arm down a little, but he couldn't get it completely unstuck. Later, when he was older, he reasoned that his arm had swollen when it got scraped and bruised on the way up. When he was five, though, all he knew was that his arm really hurt and he was trapped in the dark. And he was terrified.

The air in the linen closet smelled like his mother. It was really flowery and sweet. It wasn't a bad smell, but it made Grady's nose itch, and it reminded him of his mother . . . who wasn't here to help him. Somehow smelling her but knowing she wasn't there made everything worse.

Grady screamed and screamed and screamed. He was so, so, so scared. Why wouldn't Boone and Francis let him out? No matter how much he shrieked, they didn't come.

Grady screamed for 62 of the 373 minutes. Eventually, though, the screams, and the fact that the peanut butter had made him thirsty, closed up his throat. From that point, he could only concentrate on trying to breathe. By then, his nose was stuffed up from crying. He couldn't get a full breath of air. He thought he was going to die.

Grady didn't remember a lot about his ordeal from that point on. The only thing he could remember well was watching the big hand of his orange-faced clock move from one minute mark to the next.

According to Grady's mother, she and Grady's dad

had come home about half an hour earlier than they'd said they would. They'd found Francis and Boone asleep on the couch together. When Boone had finally admitted where he'd stashed Grady, the boy had been barely conscious. Grady hadn't spoken for days after that.

Grady never found out exactly what happened to Francis and Boone. He just knew his parents said they were "pressing charges." At the time, Grady wasn't sure what it meant, but he hoped it hurt Francis and Boone a lot.

When all was said and done, the only injury Grady got from his time in the closet was a sprained wrist and a sore throat, but the unseen damage was the real problem. He was in therapy for months before he'd let anyone close his bedroom door. He even had issues with his parents closing and locking the doors to the house. And the car was worse. Soon, any enclosed small space was a problem.

Those months had been hard on Grady and his parents. Sometimes they acted like they felt guilty about what had happened, and sometimes they acted exasperated by Grady's problems. The only good thing Grady could remember about those months was that his parents let him eat a lot of food they'd never let him have before. They'd bought him whatever candy or chips or other junk food he'd wanted. The food had distracted him from his fears. Recently, Grady's mom had told him it was her fault that he was addicted to junk food. She'd been so relieved when he'd sit in front of the TV and eat instead of freaking out about closed doors that she'd let him eat as much of it as he'd wanted.

By the time Grady had graduated from high school, Grady still loved junk food, but he was reasonably functional in most situations. He could manage small rooms and cars . . . as long as he knew he had a way to get out.

Grady blinked and looked at his candy wrapper. It was empty. He checked his watch. Ten minutes had passed. He took a shaky breath.

It had been a long time since he'd let himself think about being locked in the linen closet. Of course he'd think of it now. He looked up at the narrow, squiggly tubes. He shuddered.

Maybe he could just say that he tested it.

Grady balled up the candy wrapper and sighed. No, he couldn't do that.

Kids were going to be in those tubes. If they were defective in any way, it was Grady's job to find the defects and fix them. He wasn't going to be responsible, even partly, for anyone going through a trauma like he did when he was stuck in the closet.

Grady tucked his candy wrapper in his kit and zipped the kit's top closed. He looked at it. The tool kit wasn't going to do him much good here. If something was wrong with Ballora herself, he could use the tools to fix her, but to find out whether she functioned properly, he'd have to go through the tubes. It was going to be hard enough to squeeze his body through them without bringing his tool kit along.

Grady left it on the floor and stood. He brushed himself off and steeled himself for what he had to do.

Finally, Grady walked over to the ladder. He might as well get it over with.

Grady grasped the smooth rounded sides of the ladder and placed his foot on the first rung. He looked down at the step and was pleased to see that it was wide and had a tread for gripping the bottom of shoes. He held on to the sides of the ladder and leaned his weight backward. The ladder didn't move at all. It was sturdy. Good.

Grady tilted his head back and looked up. His resolve wavered. The ladder was tall—very tall. From this perspective, it looked like it went up and up forever. Grady could barely see the top.

Grady let go of the ladder and wiped his suddenly sweaty palms on the front of his shirt. He took a deep breath and grasped the ladder again. Before he let himself think anymore, he began climbing.

After only a dozen or so rungs, Grady was winded. After another dozen, sweat had beaded on his forehead. After another dozen, he was gasping. He had to stop. He clung to the ladder, gulping in air.

Grady looked up. He wasn't too far from the top, but his legs felt like jelly and his knees were throbbing. He snorted at the thought of Tate's "bad knees." Silently cursing his coworker, Grady ground his teeth.

Grady's annoyance gave him a burst of energy. He took a deep breath and started climbing again. This time, he forced himself to keep going until he reached the top.

When Grady crawled onto the broad rubber-floored platform at the top of the network of tubes, he was once again sucking in air. He used his shirt to wipe off his sweat-soaked face.

Grady looked at the array of tubes extending downward from the platform. He had to admit they looked plenty big enough for him to get through. Maybe this wouldn't be so bad. It was just fifty feet from the top of the tube network to the floor. It wouldn't take that long to get through it.

Grady craned his neck to examine the path of the tube nearest him. He frowned. Maybe it would take longer than he thought. The problem was that the tubes didn't just go straight down. They bent left and right and looped around, crisscrossing with other tubes, backtracking and zigzagging. The travel distance from the platform to the floor would have to be at least three or four times longer than just fifty feet.

Grady heaved a loud sigh. The sound seemed to swell around him, mocking him for his hesitation.

"Are you a man or a mouse?" Grady asked himself.

He immediately laughed. It would be better if he *was* a mouse at this point. Too bad he couldn't turn himself into one so he could scurry through the tubes double-time and get this done.

"Come on, Grady," he urged himself, "move it."

Grady edged toward the nearest tube. He peered into the opening.

Still, he hesitated.

He was just getting ready to bend down into the tube when a click and a *whoosh* startled him into immobility.

He whipped his head around and watched, wide-eyed, as the torso of Ballora, the animatronic mascot of the fitness venue, popped up out of a hole in the platform. Her long eyelashes fluttered as she turned her metal head and aimed her purple eyes at Grady.

"Hello, hello, welcome here," Ballora sang in a sweet yet raspy woman's voice. "It's time to play, nothing to fear."

Ballora's little ditty was in a minor key and dropped down at the end of each phrase. It in no way reassured him. Grady found it kind of haunting.

Ballora spun in a circle and faced Grady again. "I'm happy you're here," she purred. "I will help you get fit."

This time, she didn't sing. She just spoke. Grady liked that better.

Grady had only seen sketches of Ballora before now. She was much more impressive in person.

Ballora was an animatronic designed to look like a ballerina. In the sketches Grady had seen, Ballora "wore" a blue leotard and tutu, but this version of Ballora was just her upper body, which was attached to a robotic mechanism that moved her through the exercise venue. She was "pretty" in a weirdly robotic way. Ballora had blue hair caught up in a bun and held with what looked like a fan-shaped flamenco-dancer-style comb (all this was actually painted metal). Like most of Fazbear Entertainment's animatronics, Ballora had more teeth than Grady thought were necessary; however, the teeth were tempered somewhat by the pink blush on Ballora's sculpted cheeks.

Ballora's endoskeleton was made of a combination of metal and thick rubber-encased wires arranged to resemble musculature. Her limbs were articulated so she could move with the grace of a dancer. In most of the sketches, Ballora stood with her arms lifted gracefully over her head, but right now they were thrown out to her sides as if making a grand welcoming gesture.

"I encourage you to slide on in," Ballora began singing again. "That's the best way to begin."

Grady really didn't like Ballora's tune.

"Stop singing," Grady said. "I don't like the singing."

He was going to have to make a note of the tune to the programmers. It was far too sinister.

Ballora spun again. Her servos whirred, and when she stopped, Grady heard a metallic *clink*. He wondered if that was normal. He'd make a note of that, too.

"Please try a tube," Ballora said. "I'm here to help you get to the bottom."

"Yeah?" Grady asked doubtfully. "What can you do to help?"

"I'm here to make sure you don't get stuck."

That word made the little hairs at the back of Grady's neck stand upright. He felt them bristle against his skin. She'd just had to go and say the word *stuck*.

This was, of course, Grady's biggest fear.

Grady's heart pounded. It was taking everything he had not to scramble back to the ladder and flee from the fitness center.

Maybe he should just quit his job.

Yeah, and pay the rent with what? It had taken him months to find this job, and it was a good one.

Besides, if he didn't test the tubes, who would?

"Please give it a try," Ballora said in her soothing voice. "You can do it!"

Grady looked at Ballora. "You promise to get me out if I get stuck?"

What was he thinking? An animatronic couldn't make promises. Now wasn't a good time for Grady to change his "robots can't be trusted" mantra. Did he really want to count on this mass of metal and wires and chips—chips programmed by some misguided designer who thought horror-movie music would be encouraging to someone about to crawl into a tiny tube?

"I'll help you out if you get stuck!" Ballora assured him.

Should he believe her?

Absolutely not.

Did he have a choice if he was going do his job right?

No matter what Grady thought of animatronics, this one had to be tested. The only way to test her was to crawl into the tube.

"Okay, fine," Grady said. "I'm going."

Ballora spun again. And again, her spin ended in a sharp clinking sound.

Grady used the sound as a sort of starting gun. He crawled headfirst into the closest tube.

Grady was glad the tubes were clear. It made it easier not to feel trapped. Grady could see the way below him, and he could see the floor down beneath the tubes. He could even see the small square of black that had to be his tool kit. That black square was his true north; it was his goal. And he wanted to get to it as fast as he could.

Stretching out his arms and putting his hands together as if he was about to dive into a swimming pool, Grady slid through the tube. Gravity sucked him downward, and for a few breathless seconds, Grady was sure he was going to slip all the way to the ground. He felt pressure in his head as if he was doing a headstand. And he supposed he was, in a way.

Once, when Grady was little, an older cousin picked Grady up and hung him upside down by his feet. Being in this tube was a little like that. Grady could feel all the blood rush to his head, neck, and shoulders. It didn't feel good.

The few seconds of sliding came to an abrupt end. Grady's hands, outstretched beneath his head, encountered the first turn. Now he couldn't slide. He had to squirm.

At the turn, although it was wide enough for his body, Grady had to strain to maneuver around the corner. It was hard work. He had to push off with his knees and feet and use the power of his shoulders (what little they had) to propel himself downward.

One thing Grady could confirm already was that Ballora's Fitness & Flex lived up to its name. Working his way through the tubes was *challenging*. He could feel the tendons of his lower legs stretching, and he could feel his joints protesting motions they weren't used to. Already he was contorting his body into positions it had never gotten into before.

Grady grunted and panted as he army-crawled back and forth, but always downward, along the slick surface of the tube. He noted that the plastic's sleekness was very helpful. Getting through the tube would have been far more difficult if the surface had been made of anything that gripped. It also helped that Grady was sweating like he'd run a mile in one-hundred-degree heat. He could feel perspiration saturating his uniform shirt, and more than once, drops of sweat fell from his nose. When he inhaled, he smelled his fetid body odor. That was something else he should notate in his report. What steps would be taken to make sure these tubes didn't reek like a boys' locker room? Surely, Grady wouldn't be the only one to sweat inside these tight spaces.

Grady squirmed and skidded. He flexed, and he pulled. Twice he conked his head when he tried to lift his upper body to get more speed in his glide. Several times he whacked his elbows. He had a feeling there had to be a more graceful way to get through this sinuous maze. Maybe instruction pamphlets should be passed out before anyone got into the tubes. He imagined that instructions were given to climbers before they tried to scale a wall. The same should be true for these tunnels. Not everyone was a natural-born spelunker.

Because he hadn't noted precisely what time he'd gone into the tube, Grady didn't know exactly how long he struggled down through the winding, narrow shafts before he popped out of a tube opening and dropped onto what was marked as "Checkpoint #1." The checkpoint was a small platform with enough headspace for Grady to sit upright.

"Whew!" Grady said loudly as he wormed around on the platform and shifted onto his butt. He stretched his legs out in front of him and flexed his feet. His ankles weren't happy with him. Neither was the rest of his body. He ached in places he didn't even know he had.

Grady wiped his face with the bottom of his shirt. It didn't help much. His shirt was as damp as his face. He swiped at his eyes. His salty sweat was making them burn.

Once his eyes were clear, Grady looked around the small enclosure. Unlike the starting platform, which had been open-air, this one was inside the tube. Although it was more spacious than the tubes Grady had just gotten through, it was still confined. There was no way out of it except up or down through the tubes.

Grady tried not to think about how the platform's size resembled the floor of the linen closet. When his breathing quickened, he looked through the transparent plastic walls to remind himself the large room beyond the tube network was right there, just on the other side of the see-through wall. He'd be back in the open space soon.

Grady noticed a small plaque under the checkpoint sign. He scooted closer so he could read it. "You are one-third of the way to the bottom. Congratulations!"

"One-third?!" Grady dropped his head into his hands. He'd thought this was the halfway point.

He looked down and shook his head. "Idiot," he

admonished himself. He was clearly not halfway down. And why would it be Checkpoint #1 if the next stop was the bottom? It would just be plain old Checkpoint, or even Halfway Point.

"Wishful thinking," he muttered.

Grady licked his lips. He was really thirsty, and he wished he had some water. He figured he should add that to his list of notes. People would get thirsty in here. Maybe there should be a drinking fountain at each of the checkpoint platforms.

Not that they'd do that now. The thing was built. They weren't going to tear it apart to add plumbing to it.

Grady, however, thought this was a major design flaw. If only they'd had someone like him plan the venue. Then again, if he'd planned it, it wouldn't exist. He wouldn't have come up with something this diabolical in a million years.

And speaking of a million years, if he didn't want to spend that much time in here, he should get moving.

Grady got up on his knees and peered into the next section of tubing. When he did, his breath caught in his throat.

The tube he looked into was narrower than the one he just crawled through. He investigated a couple more tubes opening off the platform. All were smaller than what he'd already been through.

Great. Just great.

Grady rotated and dropped his head back to look up into the tube he'd just come out of. Maybe he could climb back up to the top and be done with it. The distance would be half of what he'd have to do if he kept going. Did he really need to test the whole thing? He'd already discovered its design flaws. Maybe he'd done enough. He could just wriggle his way back up to the platform.

"Yeah, but it's going *up*, dummy," he told himself.

He'd barely managed to work himself through the tube going downhill. How would he pull himself *up*?

Grady sat back on his haunches and slumped against the plastic wall of the checkpoint. He had to face facts. He didn't have the strength to climb up through the tunnels. As awful as the idea was, it would be easier to just keep going downward.

Grady took a deep breath. "Come on," he urged himself. "Get on with it."

Inching forward, Grady pushed his head and then his upper body down into the closest tube.

Although the fit in this tube was definitely tighter than in the last one Grady had been in, he could move through it. It was really tough going, though.

Whereas before Grady could push himself off the walls of the tube, here there was barely enough space for him to *be* inside the tube, much less try to contort himself into anything other than a flattened position. He had very little wriggle room. Instead of using his elbows as "treads," he had to keep his arms out in front of him and sort of writhe from side to side like an eel moving through water.

If only he *was* moving through water.

The first few bends in this narrow tube weren't too

bad. Again, Grady's perspiration helped him out. He sort of slithered along the plastic.

The first abrupt turn in the tube, however, was an issue.

It arced back in the opposite direction, requiring Grady to bend almost double to get around it. And when he bent in the middle, the tube narrowed even more. He was—just as he'd most feared—stuck.

Grady sucked in his gut and jiggled himself from side to side. He wrenched himself back and forth.

Nothing worked. He wasn't budging.

If he'd had something to grab on to, he might have been able to yank himself downward, but when he tried to grip the tube's surface, his hands slipped. His sweat wasn't in his favor now.

Grady thrashed for several minutes, getting more and more freaked out. Finally, he screamed, "Help!"

He had no idea why he was screaming. He was alone in the Pizzaplex. Not a soul could hear him.

No, wait.

What about Ballora?

In his panic, Grady had forgotten about the animatronic helper.

"Ballora!" he called out. "Help! I want out!"

When nothing happened immediately after his yell, Grady screamed again. *"Help me!"*

He was just starting to berate himself for the stupidity of trusting a robot when he heard a humming rumble coming along the tube below him. A clank sounded just a few feet from him, and then Ballora's torso snapped into view a couple feet below Grady's head. He twisted his neck to look at her.

Ballora blinked her purple eyes at him and fluttered her lashes. She spun in a circle and smiled wide enough for him to see all her teeth.

Grady's overtaxed muscles quivered. His imagination was providing him with the alarming image of Ballora using her teeth to . . .

"Don't give up now," Ballora encouraged. "You can do it. Twisting through the tunnels is good for flexibility!"

"I'm stuck!" Grady yelled. "How can I twist through the tunnels if I'm stuck?"

He once again attempted to unwedge himself from the turn in the tube. After a few seconds, he glared at Ballora. "See?"

Ballora did another spin and started to sing, "I'm so very happy to help you. I'm here to get you through."

"What did I say about the singing?" Grady growled. "Stop singing!"

Ballora held out her hands. "Here. Let me help you."

Grady wasn't keen on giving Ballora control over him, which she'd have if he let her take his hands. But what choice did he have?

Besides, Ballora was programmed to help people make it through the fitness tubes. Grady had seen her specs. She'd get him out of his predicament.

Grady stretched his arms down so Ballora could take his hands. Ballora grabbed them.

As soon as Ballora's metal fingers closed over Grady's softer ones, she clamped down. Her grip pinched his knuckles.

"Ow!" Grady complained.

Ballora ignored him. She started skimming downward through the tube, her systems thrumming deeply; the sound vibrated the tube's plastic walls.

Ballora didn't go too fast, but even so, when she tugged, Grady thought his arms were going to come out of their sockets. Sharp pains surged through his shoulders as she yanked him forward.

"That hurts!" Grady exclaimed.

Ballora still ignored him. She kept moving down, smoothly and gracefully, and as she glided easily through the tube, Grady jerked and lurched along above her.

With just one snatch, Ballora had Grady free of the turn that had seized him. However, that turn was only one of many that lay between where Grady had gotten stuck and the next checkpoint. This tube didn't seem to have any straight stretches at all. It was all twist, turn, twist, turn, loop, bend, and twist, turn.

Ballora, however, had no trouble maneuvering through the tight spaces. And she had no problem dragging Grady along with her.

It was Grady who was having the trouble. The whole procedure *hurt like hell*. Human arms weren't designed to be used as tow ropes.

Grady was certainly getting through the compact space. But at what cost?

After just a few tugs, Grady's shoulders were on fire. "Ow, ow, ow!" he chanted as Ballora hauled him along.

Following several more twists and turns, Grady's "ow"'s turned into groans and moans, and his groans quickly turned into screams. The pain in his shoulders began spreading. It radiated down his arms and up through his neck.

This was what the rack must have felt like, Grady thought, during one particularly grueling turn. His eyes were filled with tears. His breath came fast. And he was getting nauseous. The pain was unlike anything he'd ever felt before.

"Stop!" Grady finally shrieked. "Stop it!"

"Almost there," Ballora sang out.

Grady gritted his teeth and closed his eyes. He focused on his breathing. In and out, in and out. After just a few breaths, Grady found himself on another small platform.

They'd reached Checkpoint #2. Like Checkpoint #1, it was just a small platform enclosed within the tube.

Ballora let go of Grady's hands, and he immediately hugged himself. He sobbed in relief . . . and in continued torment. Just because Ballora had stopped pulling on him didn't mean Grady felt better. His shoulders were screaming bloody murder.

Grady rubbed his shoulders and rocked back and forth. He sniveled like a little kid. "It hurts!" he moaned.

Ballora did not reply.

She did not reply because she was gone. As soon as Ballora got Grady to the second checkpoint, she disappeared.

"Thank all the gods and goddesses in all the lands,"

Grady breathed out one of his RPG lines as he gingerly tried to raise and lower his arms.

He winced at the twinges of hot pain that pulsed in his shoulders. He screwed up his face. He'd probably torn a rotator cuff or something.

Grady half smiled. Now that he was sitting up and wasn't being stretched like human taffy, his sense of humor had returned. He found it funny that he might have an injury common to athletes. Grady never thought he'd tear a rotator cuff. It was far more likely he'd get carpal tunnel from too much time at the computer.

"Hey, I wonder if this will make me more appealing to women," he said out loud.

He laughed at the idea.

Was his laugh just a tad maniacal? Maybe.

He decided to stop trying to be funny. Not that he was being all that funny, anyway.

Grady leaned back against the platform wall. He continued rubbing his shoulders.

After a couple minutes, he looked down at the next set of tubes. He trembled. He really didn't think he could go through anything like that again.

And what if the next time Ballora pulled so hard, she *did* wrench his arms free of their sockets? She was a robot; she certainly had the strength to do that.

No, Grady wasn't going back into the tubes. He would wait right here on the platform, and in the morning, when Ronan and Tate saw that Grady's reports weren't filed, they'd check the venues he was supposed to test. They'd find him, and they'd get him out of here.

Grady shifted positions. The burning in his shoulders was lessening, a little.

Grady realized his face was smeared with tears and wiped them away. He sniffled, wishing he had something to blow his nose on. He also wished, again, that he had some water. And some food.

Grady looked around the platform. He frowned.

Just how would they get him out of here?

He closed his eyes and tried to remember the specs for Ballora's Fitness & Flex. Did the tunnel network have an emergency exit? Not that Grady could remember.

He was pretty sure no one had expected someone to get stuck in the tubes. He guessed the designer assumed Ballora would be able to do her job and get people out. Clearly, the designer was a complete fool. Did it not occur to that jabroni that Ballora might do the kind of damage she'd done to Grady?

"Dingus," Grady muttered.

When he got out of here, he was going to have a few words for whoever had come up with this concept—after everyone stopped laughing at him.

"Oh man," Grady moaned.

They were going to laugh at him. He could just hear the comments. He'd be the laughingstock of Fazbear Entertainment.

Grady closed his eyes and dropped his head into his hands. He was going to end up like poor Hank.

A month before, Hank—one of the engineers—had taken the Tilt-A-Whirl for a spin, and it had gotten stuck at high speed. By the time the other engineers figured out how to shut it down, Hank had spewed his entire lunch all over the ride. Somehow the press heard about the incident, and they did a front-page story with the headline: "Fazbear Entertainment Employee Tilt-A-Hurls." People were still bringing Hank barf bags on a daily basis.

Grady shook his head. No way did he want to be the famous butt of a bunch of jokes about how he was too large to get through the fitness center.

No. Grady couldn't just sit here and wait it out. He had to keep going.

Grady leaned forward so he could see the floor. The black square of his tool kit was bigger than it had been the last time he'd seen it, from the upper platform. That gave Grady hope.

It wasn't much farther. Surely, he could make it.

But what if it got even worse? Grady's muscles bunched up at the idea of being stuffed into a space even smaller than what he'd just gone through.

Grady leaned down and looked into the last set of tunnels. Some of his tension abated . . . a little.

The tunnels below Grady didn't seem to be any smaller than the ones above him. If he got through those, he could get through these. Right?

Yeah, but the only reason he got through the previous tubes was because Ballora had dragged him through them. What made him think he could do it on his own?

Grady looked down at his stomach. He drew it in as flat as he could get it.

Would it be enough to get him through to the end?

It had to be.

Grady got up on his knees. He rubbed his shoulders one last time. He took several deep beaths. Then he blew out all the air he could and dropped headfirst into the next tube.

The first few feet of the final section weren't too bad. Yes, blood still rushed to his head. Yes, he still felt the pressure in his head and shoulders. But still, Grady was heartened. He was on the last stretch. He could do this. It was going to be okay.

Grady inched his way down through the tunnel, making sure he kept his breath as slow and even as possible, moving in tiny increments so he didn't get himself wedged in any of the turns. Grady forced himself not to think about where he was and what could happen, and instead concentrated on waggling his body back and forth, like the tail of a happy dog. That motion seemed to be the most effective way to make decent progress.

Everything was going well.

And then the tubes grew even narrower.

As Grady rounded a turn, he noticed that his shoulders no longer had any room at all to waggle. The tube around him didn't feel like a tube anymore; it felt like a second skin. It hugged him like a sausage casing compressing ground pork.

Grady stopped and tried to push himself back upward. But he couldn't move. Not even a little. The tunnel squinched around him, hugging him tighter than his gran had squeezed him when he was a little kid.

Oh, how he wished his gran was here now. Any gran who could excel at hoops could figure out how to rescue her grandson from a silly plastic tube. And Grady for sure needed rescuing; he was well and truly stuck.

The memory of Ballora's "help" prominent in his mind, Grady didn't call out. He didn't want Ballora's services.

Just wait until Grady wrote up his report on the torture device masquerading as a service bot. He was going to make sure Ballora's designer never got a job in the industry again!

Grady went limp. Now he had no choice. He'd have to stay here until morning.

Maybe he'd go to sleep. He was exhausted. Sleep wasn't impossible, even in this miserable position.

Grady stiffened. But what if his circulation was being cut off?

Grady flexed his hands and his feet. He tightened and released all the muscles in his body. Good. He didn't feel any numbness or tingling. His blood flow was probably okay.

All he had to do was control his breathing.

Or no . . . he didn't even have to do that. So what if he panicked and hyperventilated? If he did that, he'd pass out. Passing out wasn't necessarily a bad thing. It was almost as good as sleep.

Grady forced himself to release the tension in his muscles. He felt tears leak from his eyes, but that was all right. Anyone in this situation would feel like crying.

But it was going to be okay. "It really is," Grady assured himself. "It's going to be fine."

Were his words tinged with just a bit of doubt? If so,

he was going to ignore it. He'd survived getting locked in the linen closet when he was five, and he'd survive this, too. He just had to wait it out.

Idly, Grady wondered how many years of therapy he'd need to get over this.

For several seconds, Grady breathed in and out, relatively calmly. But then a horrifying thought leaped to the top of his mind: What if Ballora showed up without being called?

Grady jerked his head so fast he hit it on the sides of the tunnel. He winced, but he didn't cry out. He had a feeling that he needed to be very, very quiet.

Ballora had nearly dismantled his body the first time she'd pulled him through the tunnel. He didn't even want to imagine what she'd do in this situation.

Grady returned to his concentrated breathing. But his breath caught when Ballora's voice called out, "I don't sense downward movement. Do you need my help?"

No, I don't, Grady thought.

He knew better than to respond. Any verbal reply from him might trigger Ballora's programming. She would appear and render aid when none was wanted.

Several seconds passed. Grady realized his whole body was taut. He concentrated again on relaxing.

"Do you need my help?" Ballora called out again.

Grady held his breath.

"My sensors indicate progress has stalled," Ballora reported. "Do you want my assistance?"

No, no, no, emphatically no, Grady thought. *Go do a pirouette.*

Grady exhaled as quietly as possible. Then he counted his next few breaths. He got up to seven before Ballora called out again. "I'm required to provide help to anyone who gets stuck. No one can stay stuck in Ballora's Fitness & Flex. Fitness is fun. I'm here to be sure you complete the Fitness & Flex course."

Grady held his breath again.

"Please, can I help?" Ballora called out.

Grady stayed silent.

"I want to help," Ballora persisted.

I don't care what you want, Grady thought. *I want to keep my arms intact.*

Grady breathed in and out six more times. The next breath, though, caught in his throat. Ballora's signature thrumming whir was headed his way.

When he heard the sound, Grady tried to pull his arms in. Unfortunately, they had no place to go. Grady's arms were outstretched, and his shoulders were wedged between the tube walls. His arms were dangling below him. They were ripe for the robotic picking.

Grady closed his fingers into a fist. Maybe that would make his hands less appealing to an unhelpful "helpful" robot.

Grady remained perfectly still, and he held his breath again. He closed his eyes.

A metallic clank announced that Ballora had popped up beneath him. When she did her signature spin, he felt the air current waft past his balled-up hands.

Grady continued to make like an opossum. Maybe if Ballora thought he was dead, she'd go away.

Ballora's metal hands gripped Grady's clenched ones.

Grady contorted his head to look at Ballora. "Go away!" he shouted. "I don't want your help! Get out of here!"

Ballora blinked at him, but she didn't let go of his hands. "I'm here to help," she insisted.

"I don't want your help!" Grady yelled.

He tried to free himself from Ballora's grasp by extending his fingers. She tightened her grip so he couldn't uncurl his fist.

"Let me go!" Grady screamed at her. "Go away!"

Ballora didn't go away. Instead, she started gliding downward, and she yanked Grady down with her.

The first knife thrust of pain came quickly. It speared through his shoulder sockets and thrust its way down to his shoulder blades.

Grady cried out.

"It's just a little way to the end," Ballora sang. "I'll get you around every bend."

Ballora pulled Grady below the crook in the tube that had caught him. That was admittedly a bit of a relief, but the relief didn't last long. The tubes became a series of back-and-forth turns.

Something popped in Grady's left shoulder. He screeched.

Ballora didn't care. She kept pulling.

The joint in Grady's left shoulder was out of its socket. He had felt it dislocate. The searing pain was excruciating.

Bad as it was, though, those savage sensations didn't hold his attention for long.

As Ballora went down around another turn, Grady's wrists cracked. He heard them snapping like breaking pretzels. As soon as they did, he could tell his fists were flopping at the end of his arms.

Ballora must have noticed this as well. She shifted her grip to Grady's forearms.

As soon as Ballora let go of his clenched fingers, Grady realized the fingers were broken. Actually, they weren't just broken; they were *crushed*. Ballora had clamped down so hard that she'd pulverized the fragile bones. When Grady tried to move his fingers, he could feel the bone chips grinding together.

He howled in pain and terror. How would he be able to do anything ever again with shattered fingers?

Grady didn't have long to contemplate this dismal future because his hell was just beginning. As Ballora tugged Grady down around the next twisting turn, his forearms popped free of his elbow joints. Then they, too, fractured. He heard the crunch as the bones were compressed in Ballora's grip.

Grady wasn't conscious of making sounds, but he could hear high-pitched shrieking. The shrieking seemed to be coming from far away, from someplace other than himself. But, of course, it wasn't. *He* was making those shrill sounds. The sounds of someone being mangled alive.

A whisper of a thought managed to make its way through Grady's torment: *How long could he take this level of pain? Wouldn't he pass out soon?*

Ballora came to a stop when Grady got stuck in the

tightest corner he'd encountered yet. When she did, she shifted her grip to above his elbows. His upper arms broke. He yowled.

Ballora jiggled Grady back and forth. He felt his ribs give way. The sensation was like having a molten hot band of metal cinched around him.

And still, he didn't pass out.

In the next turn, Grady's hip sockets let go of his leg bones. As they did, Grady realized, through the black miasma of his pain, that he wasn't going to pass out. He was upside down. Most of his blood was pooled in his head. His brain was well-supplied with what it needed to keep trucking along. And his brain didn't care that the rest of him was enduring more pain than the human body was designed to handle. It didn't care that Ballora's determined trek through the tube was deconstructing Grady's skeletal structure joint by joint, bone by bone. It didn't care that Grady was being twisted and compressed into something not unlike the pretzels he so loved.

Before the next curve in the tube, Ballora repositioned her grip once again. As she did, one of her metal fingers impaled Grady's left eye. Grady keened and heaved. He upchucked his candy bar; the vomit poured into the tube. Ballora slid him down through the mess.

The sickly sweet and slightly acidic odor of his vomit hit his nose, and he threw up again. But then he couldn't smell anything anymore. Ballora's rescue efforts on the next series of pleat-like turns pressed his face so hard against the side of the tube that his nose cracked.

Grady felt warmth course over his cheek. He knew his

now-eyeless socket was gushing blood, but he couldn't do anything about it. He couldn't do anything about anything. All Grady could do was scream and cry as he felt his body break apart.

"Why don't you have one of those hide-a-key rocks?" Tate asked as Ronan signaled to turn into the employee parking lot at the back of the Pizzaplex.

Ronan didn't think he had to explain anything to Tate. The guy didn't have any right to complain that they had to come back for Ronan's house keys. Ronan gave Tate a ride every day, and Tate never paid for gas; yet, when Ronan wanted to turn around and go back for his keys, Tate had the nerve to ask Ronan to go the remaining five miles to Tate's apartment building before returning to the Pizzaplex. Ronan had ignored him and made a U-turn.

For the last half hour, Tate had been grousing. "It's bad enough we have a forty-five-minute commute to start with. Now we have to go back and do nearly all of it again?"

"Those fake rocks aren't safe," Ronan told Tate now. "Burglars know about them, and they look for them before they bother to break into a home. I read an article about it."

Tate rolled his eyes. "Whatever." He stared sullenly out the passenger window.

Ronan pulled his minivan into his assigned parking spot, two down from Grady's. Grady's old pickup was still there. Obviously, he hadn't yet finished up his safety checks.

Ronan concentrated on positioning the minivan

precisely between the lines. When he was satisfied, he put the transmission in park.

Tate frowned and looked pointedly at the hundred yards between Ronan's spot and the employee entrance. "Why are you parking all the way over here?"

Ronan turned off the minivan. "This is my spot," he explained patiently.

Tate threw up his hands. "But there's no one around! You could just pull up to the curb." He pointed toward the employee entrance.

Ronan raised an eyebrow. "That's a no-parking zone." Ronan opened his car door. "Come on."

Tate gave Ronan a look. "Why do I have to go with you? Just leave the keys and I'll hang here and listen to tunes."

Ronan threw Tate's look right back at him. "I may look big and dumb, but I'm not. I'm not leaving you with the keys to ol' Betty. Come on." Ronan gave Tate his best glare. His sister, Rhonda, had told him he looked terrifying when he did that. She thought it was "a hoot" because she knew Ronan didn't even like swatting mosquitoes. But Rhonda must have been right about it because people tended to do whatever Ronan wanted when he gave them the glare. Tate, despite being one of the laziest people Ronan had ever met, was no exception.

Tate grumbled and got out of the minivan. Ronan carefully locked it up, and the two men headed toward the employee entrance.

"You're one weird dude," Tate told Ronan.

If Ronan had gotten a dollar for every time Tate had

said that to him, he'd have enough money to buy yarn for the shawl he wanted to knit for his mother. Tate couldn't seem to get over the fact that Ronan was both a body-builder and a knitter, that he was in a local fight club and also owned a minivan named Betty so he could drive his knitting club members to textile conventions and knit-a-longs. Ronan, however, couldn't care less what Tate thought of him—or what anyone thought of him, for that matter.

"Can we hurry it up?" Tate asked, trotting out ahead of Ronan. "I told you I'm supposed to meet Karen at the lake. Now I'm going to be late."

"You're always late. She'll expect it," Ronan said. He didn't pick up his pace.

"That's low, dude," Tate said.

Ronan ignored him. He dug his Pizzaplex keys out of his pants pocket and had them ready when they reached the door.

Tate rushed through the door ahead of Ronan as soon as Ronan unlocked the door and deactivated the alarm, and Tate bounced like a kid who needed to pee while Ronan locked the door behind them and reactivated the alarm. "Could you be any slower?" Tate complained.

Ronan pocketed his Pizzaplex keys again and put his hands on his hips. "I'm sure I can."

Tate exhaled loudly, but he didn't speak again as they strode through the gray double doors leading to the employee break room. Tate meandered into the break room, heading toward the cubbyholes where they were supposed to leave their reports at the end of the day. Tate was probably going to look at Ronan's and Grady's to compare their progress with his own. Tate was lazy, but he was also strangely competitive.

Ronan headed into the dingy locker room. With its beige paint job and low-wattage light bulbs, it was a surprising contrast to all the screamingly bright colors and lights in the main part of the Pizzaplex. Ronan figured Fazbear Entertainment didn't want to spend any more money than necessary on their employees. He couldn't really complain, though. His salary was good. This job had given him the down payment to buy his first house. He had no beef with Fazbear Entertainment; they could paint their locker rooms any boring color they wanted.

Ronan opened his locker and rummaged around behind his tool kit. He kept his house keys in his backpack, which he'd grabbed when he and Tate had left. His keys, however, must have slipped out when he'd gotten his lunch from his pack earlier in the day. Yep. There they were. They'd fallen behind his spare uniform shirt.

Ronan grabbed the keys and closed his locker. He turned.

"Hey, Ronan," Tate called. "Come here a second."

Ronan strode into the employee break room. He found Tate rifling through Grady's paperwork. Just as Ronan had suspected.

"Why are you looking at Grady's stuff?" Ronan asked . . . as if he didn't know.

Tate didn't answer the question. He waved a sheaf of paper. "Did you know he was going to do Ballora's next? I thought he was going to do that next week, but he scheduled it for today."

Ronan gave Tate a "What's your point?" look.

Tate grinned. "He's probably down there right now. Can you imagine him squeezing through those tubes?" He whooped in laughter. Tate stuffed Grady's papers back in their slot. "Come on. Let's go check on him."

Ronan raised both eyebrows. "I thought you were in a hurry. You said you were going to be late."

Tate waved away the idea. "I'm already late. What's it matter if I'm a little bit later? Karen can wait."

Karen has terrible taste in men, Ronan thought. He'd met Karen. She was cute and seemed sweet. What did she see in Tate?

"All right," Ronan said. He had no trouble with checking on Grady. He'd been reluctant to leave Grady alone in the first place. He didn't like breaking the rules. But Grady had insisted, and Ronan had wanted to get home. He'd planned on making some hummus dip and homemade whole-wheat pita bread for the knitting club meeting. Now he wouldn't have time for the bread, but he could still do the dip . . . even if he and Tate took a few minutes to go down to Ballora's.

"Even if I didn't have bad knees," Tate was saying as they walked to the main concourse, "I still wouldn't have done Ballora's. Those tunnels are too small, and I don't even have claustrophobia or anything, not like Grady."

"Grady doesn't have claustrophobia," Ronan said. "He has cleithrophobia."

Tate ignored him. "Whatever."

"It's the fear of being trapped," Ronan explained. "People with claustrophobia don't like small spaces, whether they're trapped or not. People with cleithrophobia can tolerate small spaces as long as they know they can come and go. They're afraid of being stuck."

Tate raised an eyebrow. "How do you know all that?"

Ronan shrugged. "I read."

Ronan lengthened his stride, and Tate trotted to keep up.

"But why do you know that's what Grady has?" Tate asked.

Ronan flicked a glance at Tate. "I listen."

Tate didn't answer. He probably hadn't even gotten the dig. He was looking at the darkened entrance to the Role Play area. He waved a hand toward it. "In the morning, I'll be checking the sets in there. Can't wait to see what they've done with the Fazbear's Fright Haunted House. I was so stoked when I saw it on the specs."

Not for the first time, Ronan wondered how Tate managed to do his job. Not that he did it that well. Ronan and Grady both had covered for Tate too many times to count. Tate's work was haphazard and incomplete. The man's mind was like a squirrel. It was constantly darting from here to there and back again. And eventually it led back around to their previous conversation. "Who *would* want to be trapped?"

Ronan didn't bother to answer what he figured was a rhetorical question. He kept his gaze straight ahead, making sure he didn't look at the swings. In the faint security lights, the swings looked too much like a giant squid to suit Ronan. Ronan didn't like squids. They were gushy. Ronan didn't like gushy.

Ronan's mother often teased him about how he had a

soft stomach when it came to things like squids or slugs or worms and anything having to do with the inside of the human body. "Rock-hard abs on the outside and soft and gooey on the inside," she always teased him.

Tate jogged out ahead of Ronan in the long red hallway that lead to Ballora's. When they reached the stairs, he perched his bony butt on the railing and slid down it, hopping onto the floor at the bottom before Ronan got halfway down the long flight.

Tate did a funky little dance to music only he could hear. He looked up the stairs. "Come on, slowpoke."

Ronan shot Tate his patented glare, but Tate was too busy spinning on one foot to notice. Ronan trotted down the last few steps, and Tate stopped dancing. Together, they headed into the curved yellow hallway of Ballora's Fitness & Flex.

When they were just halfway around the curve, they knew Grady was indeed in the fitness venue. Ballora's entrance was fully lit. Its archway was illuminated like the sparkling marquee of a Broadway show. Beyond the entrance, all the lights in the venue were on, too.

Tate trotted through the archway. "Yo, Grady!" he called out. "Dude! Hope you're not stuck!"

Ronan shook his head. He sighed and followed his uncouth coworker into Ballora's. He didn't notice that Tate had stopped until he literally plowed into him. "Sorry," Ronan said automatically as Tate stutter-stepped forward and windmilled his arms to keep his balance.

Tate didn't say anything. Which was weird. Tate always had something to say.

Ronan looked at Tate, and he quickly lifted his head to follow the direction of Tate's wide-eyed stare.

The second Ronan looked upward, he wished he hadn't.

He saw what had grabbed Tate's attention immediately. It was impossible to miss.

Ronan leaned over and covered his mouth. He felt faint, so he went to his knees. His breath was coming fast. The room started to spin.

Tate crouched down next to him. "Tuck your head, big guy. Breathe slow." Tate draped an arm over Ronan's shoulder. "Just take a minute."

Because Ronan didn't want to think about what he'd seen, he focused on Tate's out-of-character compassion. He'd never known Tate to be so nice. Why wasn't he acting like his usual jerky self?

Tate patted Ronan's back. "That's it. Keep breathing slowly. Look at me."

Ronan tried to do as instructed as he turned toward his coworker. Tate, however, wasn't looking at Ronan. He was staring at the tubes behind the transparent wall.

Ronan thought about what he'd just seen inside one of those tubes. His stomach heaved. He clapped a hand over his mouth.

Poor Grady.

It *was* Grady, wasn't it?

Ronan couldn't bring himself to look again.

"Is it Grady?" Ronan asked Tate.

"Who else would it be?" Tate snapped.

Ah, there was the Tate whom Ronan knew so well.

"But he's . . ." Ronan stopped. He didn't want to speak out loud about the mangled, twisted, broken limbs and torso that used to be Grady. Seeing it had been bad enough. Talking about it would somehow make it worse.

Ronan wondered if he'd ever erase from his mind the image of Grady's wrecked body suspended upside down in the tube, tucked back and forth—unthinkably—in a tight series of the tube's zigzags. How would Ronan ever forget Grady's misshapen face with its one remaining good eye plastered against the plastic? He was sure he'd never be able to wipe from his memory banks Grady's empty socket or the eyeball dangling from one of Ballora's metal fingers. And he would be forever tormented by the image of Grady's five-foot-six-inch frame elongated into nearly twice that length . . . Grady's body now so deconstructed that it was strewn through the tube.

"What happened?!" Ronan asked. It was a stupid question, of course. It was clear, even in the few seconds he'd looked at Grady's disfigured body, what had happened. Clearly, Ballora's designer hadn't included a fail-safe, some command that told her getting unstuck was less important than making sure the person she was helping wasn't injured. The robot was outrageously flawed.

"This is bad," Tate said.

Ronan wanted to say something sarcastic, but it wasn't appropriate. He swallowed and licked his lips. "I didn't look long enough," he said. "And I can't—I can't look again. Is he alive?"

Tate took a few steps toward the transparent wall.

Ronan watched Tate but didn't look beyond him to the tube again.

Tate squinted at the tube. "I don't know. It's hard to see whether he's breathing."

Ronan's stomach flipped over. He dropped his head. His eyes moistened.

He and Grady hadn't been close or anything; they were just coworkers. But Grady had been a nice guy. And nice guy or not, no one deserved to die like *that*.

Tate inhaled sharply.

Ronan's head snapped up. "What?"

Tate took another step toward the tubes. "Oh man," he said. "I think I just saw him blink."

Ronan groaned. He couldn't even imagine—didn't want to imagine—what Grady was feeling.

In the too-long glimpse he'd gotten of Grady, Ronan had seen that not only were Grady's limbs contorted into impossible positions, but his uniform was saturated with blood. Many of his bone breaks must have been compound fractures. Ronan could only guess . . . not that he wanted to . . . at how many times Grady's shattered bones had jabbed through his skin.

"Yeah," Tate said. "He just did it again. He's alive."

Tate sounded calm, but his voice was tight. Ronan found it absurdly comforting that Tate was affected by what he was looking at. Maybe the guy wasn't as shallow as Ronan had thought. Although, Tate *was* looking directly at the bloody, crimped-up Grady as if gawking at an exhibit in a zoo.

Ronan forced himself to stand. He had to concentrate to make sure his legs held him up.

"We need to get him out of there," Ronan said.

Tate slowly turned and goggled at Ronan. "And just how are we going to do that? We have no way to get into those tubes."

"We need to call 911." Ronan reached into his pocket and pulled out his phone. Before he could lift it, though, Tate plucked it from his hand.

"Dude," Tate said, clutching the phone, "what are you *thinking?*"

"I'm thinking we need to get him out of there, and if we can't do it, we need to get someone here who can."

Tate shook his head. "We can't do that."

Ronan raised both eyebrows. "What in the world do you mean?"

Tate didn't answer. He looked back at Grady.

"Give me my phone." Ronan tried to grab it.

Tate hopped out of reach. "I can't do that, dude."

Ronan tried his glare.

Tate shook his head. "You don't get it. If we call someone, it's going to come out that we left him here alone. Totally against the rules."

"That's what I said earlier."

"Yeah, I know. But no matter what you said, we left him. And this happened." He waved toward the tubes. Ronan didn't look in the direction of the gesture.

"Obviously, this venue is totally screwed up if this happened," Tate went on. "If Grady survives, he would have no problem making a worker's comp claim. Heck, he . . . or most likely his family, because I don't see how he can survive that"—Tate waved his hand at the tubes—"might even be able to sue Fazbear Entertainment. If an injury is intentional, an employee or surviving family can sue, and intentional is defined as having certain knowledge an injury would occur and willfully disregarding that knowledge."

Ronan stared at Tate open-mouthed. "How do you know all that?"

Tate shrugged. "My old man's a lawyer."

No kidding.

Ronan shook his head. "But Fazbear Entertainment couldn't have known for sure someone would get injured in there." He waved in the direction of the tubes.

Tate snorted. "Are you kidding me?" He, too, gestured at the tubes. "Do you see the size of those lower tubes? No way a full-size man can make it through those. And yet, they wanted one of us to test it. They had to have known we'd get hurt. It wouldn't be hard to make a case."

Ronan rubbed his forehead. "Okay. Fine. But that means they deserve to be sued. Why can't we get him out?"

Tate turned his back to the tubes and stood right in front of Ronan. When he spoke again, his voice was even, and he spoke slowly as if explaining algebra to a ten-year-old. "Grady's injuries are a liability nightmare. What do you think Fazbear Entertainment is going to do with the two employees who left Grady here by himself to get stuck?"

Ronan thought hard. Even if they'd stayed, they wouldn't

have been with Grady. He still could have gotten stuck. He opened his mouth to say that, but Tate spoke first.

"And even if we argued that it would have happened anyway, we broke protocol and the result was disastrous. They'd have clear grounds to fire us. And I don't know about you, but I don't want to get fired."

Ronan thought about what would happen with his new mortgage payment if he lost his job. No, he didn't want to get fired, either.

But was his new house more important than another human's life? Obviously not.

"Even so," Ronan said, "we have to help him. He's . . ." His voice broke. He couldn't even find the words to describe it.

"Yeah, I know," Tate said. "I know." He, too, cleared his throat. "But look at him—the minute anyone tries to move him, he's going to be in excruciating pain, and he'll bleed out before they can get him to the hospital. There's no way he can survive."

Ronan had a terrible thought. "But if he's blinking, that means he's conscious, and . . ." He couldn't say it.

"And yeah, he's probably in horrible pain. I get it. But then again, maybe not. Look at how his spine is all screwed up. Maybe he's paralyzed. There's no way to tell," Tate said. "That blinking could just be a reflex or something."

Ronan didn't look at Grady's spine. He latched on to the hope that Grady couldn't feel any of the agony wracking his body.

"You really think so?" Ronan asked.

Tate nodded vehemently. "I really do."

Ronan chewed on his lower lip.

As if sensing Ronan's indecision, Tate moved in and put a hand on Ronan's forearm. "This sucks the big one. It really does. But Grady might as well be dead. And anything we do to help him right now is going to get us in really big trouble. There's no upside to us calling anyone. Not for Grady, and not for us. He's gone, whether dead or soon to be. Maybe he wasn't even blinking. Maybe it was just a death spasm. And I bet he'd be the first one to say there's no point in us throwing away good jobs and maybe even our careers by letting anyone know we let him stay here."

Ronan kept chewing on his lip. Tate was making sense. But this was Tate, one of the most self-interested people Ronan had ever meant. Who cared if *Tate* made sense?

Then again, what would be the point in losing their jobs if Grady was already dead, or if he wouldn't survive the extraction?

Ronan thought about his nice house and his lovely friends in the knitting club. He thought about all the luscious yarn he'd recently bought because his pay was so good. Did he want to give all that up?

Tate gripped Ronan's arm. "Listen, all we have to do is walk away. We leave. The CCTV isn't installed yet, so they're not tracking us. We'll just say that we all left at quitting time like usual. Grady must have come back on his own. We didn't know about it."

Ronan lifted his head and forced himself to look at Grady again. If he was going to abandon a dying man, the least he could do was acknowledge the man before he left.

Ronan had to cover his mouth again when his gaze landed on Grady's misshapen and bloody form. He clutched his stomach, sure he was going to heave.

"Keep it together, big guy," Tate said softly.

Ronan brushed away tears and looked into Grady's one remaining eye. The eye looked back at Ronan, unblinking. Ronan noticed that Grady's brown iris was cloudy. Was he dead already? No, the eye twitched. He was still alive.

What was Grady thinking as he stared out at his coworkers? *Was* he thinking? Would a man in that condition still have rational thought? If Grady was thinking, Ronan couldn't tell. Grady's face was so smashed that no expression was possible. Was Grady hoping they'd save him, or was he wishing they'd go and let him die?

Ronan dropped his gaze. "Bye, Grady," he whispered.

Tate took Ronan's arm and turned him away from the tubes. Gently, Tate led Ronan out of Ballora's.

Ronan half closed his eyes against the blinding lights of Ballora's archway as Tate ushered him into the yellow hallway. He didn't let himself think about what they were walking away from. Instead, he concentrated on making his legs work. He focused on breathing in and out.

"All we have to do," Tate said as they followed the

curved hallway, heading toward the stairs, "is come into work as usual in the morning. He'll be dead by then."

Grady's remaining eye watched his coworkers. They disappeared around the corner of the yellow hallway.

He hadn't been able to hear everything Ronan and Tate had said. Even though his ears still worked—they were the only body parts that had avoided massive trauma—the tube and the transparent wall muted sound. He had, however, heard enough.

Grady had wanted to cry even more than he already had when Tate had hypothesized that Grady was paralyzed. If only. Yes, Grady's spine was broken, but somehow, his nerve endings were functioning just fine. The totality of his body was one throbbing mass of indescribable suffering.

Grady couldn't hate his coworkers for leaving him to die. He'd probably have done the same thing if he'd been in their place. He needed this job just as badly.

But he wished they'd stayed with him a little while longer.

Ballora, who had been silently pulling on Grady the whole time Ronan and Tate had been standing there talking, spoke up. "You're stuck. I'll help you."

She yanked harder, and Grady heard a series of wet pops and two cracks. New waves of pain sluiced through Grady's arms and cascaded through his whole body.

Grady couldn't even protest the assault on his system. Even if he could have, he wouldn't have. He was dying, and the only company he had was Ballora. He wouldn't have sent her away now, for anything.

If Grady had to die trapped in his worst nightmare, he didn't want to do it alone. Even Ballora's cold and unfeeling grip was better than nothing.

Ballora spoke up one more time. "You're stuck. I want to help."

ABOUT THE
AUTHORS

Scott Cawthon is the author of the bestselling video game series *Five Nights at Freddy's*, and while he is a game designer by trade, he is first and foremost a storyteller at heart. He is a graduate of the Art Institute of Houston and lives in Texas with his family.

Kelly Parra is the author of YA novels *Graffiti Girl*, *Invisible Touch*, and other supernatural short stories. In addition to her independent works, Kelly works with Kevin Anderson & Associates on a variety of projects. She resides in Central Coast, California, with her husband and two children.

Andrea Rains Waggener is an author, novelist, ghost-writer, essayist, short story writer, screenwriter, copywriter, editor, poet, and a proud member of Kevin Anderson & Associates' team of writers. In a past she prefers not to remember much, she was a claims adjuster, JCPenney's catalog order taker (before computers!), appellate court clerk, legal writing instructor, and lawyer. Writing in genres that vary from her chick-lit novel, *Alternate Beauty*, to her dog how-to book, *Dog Parenting*, to her self-help book, *Healthy, Wealthy, & Wise*, to ghostwritten memoirs to ghostwritten YA, horror, mystery, and mainstream fiction projects, Andrea still manages to find time to watch the rain and obsess over her dog and her knitting, art, and music projects. She lives with her husband and said dog on the Washington Coast, and if she isn't at home creating something, she can be found walking on the beach.

The footsteps that had prompted Lucia and her friends (and not-friends) to cower among dusty, caved-in cardboard boxes in a dark, musty storeroom were unlike any footsteps Lucia had heard before. Measured and steady, the steps hit the hallway's linoleum flooring with a bizarre combination of grace and heaviness. The steps were precise taps, barely touching the floor before moving on. At the same time, the steps were weighty. Each tap created a vibration that juddered the storeroom. That reverberation was a disturbing reminder that just a thin wall separated Lucia and the others from whatever was stalking down the hallway outside the door that Adrian had just locked.

"What . . . ?" Joel began.

"Shhh," Lucia admonished.

Joel glared at Lucia, but he closed his mouth. He pressed his full lips together so hard they lost color.

Putting his massive shoulders back and puffing up his chest, Joel made an attempt at swag, but his pale lips, wide eyes, and filthy bright purple-and-yellow T-shirt made it impossible for him to even approximate stylish confidence. He swallowed hard, and his pronounced Adam's apple bobbed up and down.

Lucia returned her attention to the footsteps. Like Joel and the others, she faced the door. She stiffened as the footsteps' cadence slowed . . . just a few feet from the storeroom door.

Adrian silently widened his stance and pressed his back hard against the door. He braced his hands against the door's scarred red metal.

Just as silently, using the light-on-his-feet talents that made him a great cheerleader, Nick stepped over to join Adrian. He, too, pressed his hands against the door. His triceps muscles bulged.

Clearly, Adrian and Nick were as unwilling to face whatever was outside the storeroom as Lucia was. Glancing at the others, Lucia realized her unease was shared by everyone.

Hope, who usually looked perky and pristine in any situation, was disheveled and smudged. Her big eyes nearly consumed her pale face. She clutched at her friend Kelly, whose brows were bunched over her pretty, slanted eyes.

Not bothering with posturing like his buddy Joel, Wade was backed against a stack of boxes. His broad shoulders were curled inward, and his head was tucked like he was bracing for a tackle. As a quarterback who'd endured dozens of sacks, he had the posture down

Lucia couldn't see the last of their group, Jayce, because he stood behind her. But she could feel his staccato breaths falling against the kinky curls on top of her head. She could smell his breath, too; the funnel cake he'd eaten at the carnival had left a sickly sweet residue that had been soured by his fear.

The carnival. How long ago had they left its bright lights and cheery music? *Just a couple hours*, Lucia thought. It seemed like days.

The footsteps stopped completely. Right outside the door. Everyone held their breaths.

The already barely-there light in the storage room blinked out. Blackness engulfed them.

Behind Lucia, Jayce gasped. Lucia winced at the sound. She stared hard into the darkness, listening for even a hint of movement outside the door.

One second. Two seconds. Three seconds.

The dim light returned. It was flickering, but it stayed on.

Lucia realized she was still counting seconds, and she stopped. The counting somehow made the terror grow. And knowing how many seconds were passing wasn't going to stop whatever was about to happen.

As soon as Lucia stopped counting, the footsteps started up again. The taps were wrapped in three other nerve-racking sounds—each tap came with a hiss, a metallic creak, and a grating rasp. Lucia didn't even want to try to imagine what could make that kind of sound. She could tell by the others' taut expressions that they felt the same way.

Trying not to count, and failing, Lucia started up again and got to twenty-seven before Adrian removed his hands from the door. Nick followed suit. Everyone remained deathly quiet for another full minute. Then Adrian carefully walked away from the door.

Lucia noticed that the storage room light was steady again. Dim, but steady.

Motioning for the others to follow him, Adrian stepped behind two stacks of boxes. The stacks were set apart from at least a dozen similar stacks. Most of the boxes were sealed, but the ones that were open revealed colorful paper cups and plates, pizza pans and boxes, and small toys, probably intended as prizes for the arcade games. All the boxes were sagging as if deflated by years of moisture, but they felt dry now. In fact, they were almost brittle. As Lucia brushed against a flapping box lid, it crackled like a dried leaf.

Adrian led the group through the maze of boxes, their feet smudging the dust that covered the black-and-white-checkered floor, their steps occasionally scattering the husks of dead flies and cockroaches. Lucia hoped the cockroaches came after the pizzeria closed. The dust filled the air with a grittiness that smelled vaguely like stale bread, and it was drying out Lucia's nose and mouth.

When they reached the back corner of the storage room, Adrian turned and faced them. "We need to find a way out of here," he whispered.

"You think?" Joel said at full volume.

"Shhh," everyone hissed at him.

Joel held up his oversize, rubbery-looking hands in surrender. He shrugged and tried the swag thing again. It wasn't any more successful than his first attempt.

"We already looked for a way out, Adrian," Hope protested. She pressed against his side.

Adrian put his arm around her. "I know, babe, but we weren't careful about it. We were a little . . ."

"Panicked?" Jayce suggested.

"Hit or miss," Adrian said. "I think we could be more thorough."

"We could also try harder to get through the barriers we found," Lucia whispered.

"If I can't move it," Joel said, again at full volume, "it can't be moved."

Joel got another chorus of "shhh." Lucia rolled her eyes.

"We should do a more thorough search for something to pry away the barriers," Adrian said. "And we should look for ways out we might have missed the first time around."

No one protested, but no one jumped into action, either. Lucia felt the hair on the back of her neck bristle at the very thought of leaving the storage room.

"I also think we should split up," Adrian said. "We need to find a way out fast. Searching in four teams will speed up the process."

Now everyone else spoke up. In whispers (with the exception of the clueless Joel), they all talked at once.

"Is that a good idea?" Lucia asked. She thought it strange that no one was bringing up the elephant in the room. Who—or what—had walked past the store-room door?

"Me and Wade will buddy up," Joel said.

"I'm with Joel," Wade said.

"I'd like to pair with Lucia," Kelly said.

"I'm with you, Adrian," Jayce said.

"I'm staying with you, hon," Hope said to Adrian.

"We can team up, Hope," Nick said.

Lucia quickly parsed the overlapping words. She blinked at Kelly. Why did Kelly want to partner up with Lucia?

Adrian, who apparently had decided he was in charge (but he did it in a non-obnoxious way), pointed at the others in turn. "Hope, go with Nick. You two are used to working together as a team."

Hope's face crumpled for a nanosecond; then she smiled at Nick. She and Nick were the heads of the school's cheerleading squad. They did work well together. She nodded.

"Jayce and I will pair up," Adrian continued. "Lucia, are you good with Kelly?"

"Sure." Lucia was actually happy to be paired with Kelly. She'd always wanted to get to know the girl better. And she was sure Kelly would be more useful in a crisis than Jayce would be. If Adrian hadn't chosen Jayce to partner with, Jayce, as Lucia's date, would have wanted to be with Lucia.

"And Joel's with Wade," Adrian finished.

The two overgrown boys nodded.

"Okay," Adrian said. "Let's make a plan. Jayce, can I have your tablet and a pen?"

For the next several minutes, the group argued over creating a map of the abandoned restaurant they were trapped in. Even though they'd been together when they'd raced around the place trying to find a way out, they disagreed on which rooms were where. It took a few heated exchanges before Jayce finally took the tablet and pen back from Adrian and drew, at almost the speed of light, a detailed map of the dilapidated pizzeria. And of course, because he had an artist's eye, the map was perfect.

"Thanks, Jayce," Adrian said when Jayce handed him the map. "Okay. Let's do it this way. Jayce and I will take the main dining room, arcade, lobby, and party rooms."

"But that's where the body parts are," Jayce squeaked.

"I've got your back," Adrian said.

Jayce frowned but nodded.

"Hope," Adrian continued, "you and Nick take the stage, backstage area, and kitchen area."

Hope and Nick gave Adrian a similar frown and nod.

"Joel and Wade, explore the employees' lounge and the other storage room and the furnace room. Lucia and Kelly, do a thorough search of the main restrooms, the maintenance room, the room that had all those robotic parts, and the office at the end of the front hall." As he talked, Adrian tapped the appropriate parts of Jayce's map.

When he was done, no one said anything. And no one moved.

Jayce cleared his throat. He looked up at Adrian. "Um, are we going to ignore what we just heard or what?"

Lucia looked at Jayce with newfound admiration. Finally, someone was willing to speak about the unspeakable.

Adrian rubbed his perfect jaw. His finger rested on the slight indentation in his square chin. After a couple seconds, he said, "Sometimes talking about things just makes them worse."

Kelly, surprisingly, spoke up. "I agree. I'm sure we all have theories, but if we get into them, they're not going to help us get out of here. They'll probably just get us all worked up and freaked out. Then we'll be too scared to go out there." She pointed toward the storeroom door.

Adrian flashed Kelly his best grin. "Couldn't have said it better. And the reason I think pairing off is the best thing to do is because a pair can move around more stealthily than a group of eight. It goes without saying that we all need to stay alert for . . . whatever we heard."

When they'd hesitantly opened the storage room door, Lucia had exhaled in unison with the others when they found the hallway empty. Without discussing it, they all split into their assigned pairs. Even Joel appeared to understand the need for silence as he and Wade crossed the hallway and headed toward the employee's lounge. A few feet back toward the dining room, Nick and Hope paused by one of the two swinging doors leading into and out of the kitchen. Hope blew a kiss to Adrian, and then she and Nick slipped into the kitchen. Hope's face was taut, her brave smile strained. Nick's expression was blank, focused.

Adrian, Jayce, Kelly, and Lucia went farther down the hall, heading toward the dining room. Every step they took through the dimly lit hallway raised Lucia's blood pressure a bit higher. Her brain was replaying, in disturbing Technicolor, all the body parts they'd found in that room. Every cell in Lucia's body was trying to turn her around and point her in any direction but the direction they were going, but she overrode their wisdom and pushed on.

Once they reached the shadowy, cluttered dining room, however, Lucia was happy to do her group's bidding. They urged her to pick up the pace, and she took off at a jog toward the archway leading to the lobby. Kelly apparently agreed that the dining room wasn't the place to be. She trotted alongside Lucia as they weaved around broken tables and chairs and the inexplicable piles of broken robotic endoskeletons. They were both careful to avoid the areas they knew held decaying body parts.

When they eventually reached the red-and-yellow-walled entrance to the restaurant, they paused. Glancing around the lobby to be sure it was empty (thankfully, it was), they turned in unison and looked down the main hallway, which ran toward the end of the building opposite the dining room and arcade.

Lucia and the others had been so out of their minds with the shock of finding the body parts that when they'd run down this hall toward a glowing red exit sign, Lucia had barely registered her surroundings. Now Lucia was more alert, more aware of what was nearby. So she noted the faded, peeling posters that lined the hall's red walls.

Kelly leaned toward Lucia and whispered in Lucia's ear, "Those were the original animatronic characters. Right?"

Lucia gazed at the posters, which depicted a top hat-wearing brown bear, a blue bunny cradling a guitar, a bright yellow chick holding a toothy cupcake poised on a plate, and a pirate fox sporting a black eye patch and a hook in place of one hand. Lucia nodded.

Together, she and Kelly took a tentative step down the hall. Both of them looked left and right constantly. They threw in frequent glances over their shoulders, too. Lucia was thankful that her partner was as diligently vigilant as Lucia was.

Like all the other areas of the restaurant, the hallway was lit, but the light wasn't bright. Flickering light bulbs created pockets of pale yellow and murky gray along the checkered-floored corridor. Lucia concentrated on the dark doorways that were spaced along the hallway. She remembered from their earlier quick search for an exit, and from Jayce's map, that the first two doorways led to restrooms. The next one opened into a maintenance supply room. Beyond that was the robotic Parts and Service Room. And at the end of the hall, just before the exit that was completely blocked by concrete blocks and heavy, metal endoskeletons, a small office sat shrouded in murky half-light.

"Restrooms first?" Kelly asked.

Lucia nodded. Together, they walked forward and

eased open the soiled yellow door that was marked LADIES. They stepped into a room lined on one side by white sinks stained brown by dirt and dust and on the other by a row of disconcertingly dark stalls with closed red metal doors. Because the restroom was even gloomier than the hallway, Lucia couldn't see under the stall doors. Anything could have been lurking behind them.

Lucia exchanged a look with Kelly, who pointed at the first closed stall door. Together, they took mincing steps toward it.

"Yo, dude," Joel said, reaching into one of the black metal lockers lining the back wall of the employees' lounge. "Check this out." He held up something small and rectangular. "It's a pager! How's that for a blast from the past?"

Wade, who had been trying to loosen a vent cover on the other side of the room, lifted his head and scowled at his friend. "Could you keep it down?" he scolded in a loud whisper.

Joel grumbled and flipped closed the locker he'd been rifling through. The metallic slap echoed through the room. Wade cringed and shook his head.

Wade and Joel had been friends for two years, since they both got on the varsity football team. Sometimes though, Wade wasn't so sure friends was the right word to describe their relationship. The truth was they didn't have a lot in common. Football was pretty much it. But that didn't stop them from hanging out together all the time. Once in a great while, usually when he was feeling sorry for himself because his dad had smacked him around, Wade was willing to admit that he and Joel spent all their time together because neither of them had any other real friends. Most of the time, though, Wade just pretended he chose Joel as his best buddy . . . and he put up with his friend's frequent stupidity.

Wade wasn't in the mood to tolerate it at the moment, though. He wanted out of this place.

"Do you want to try to make some more noise?" Wade flung at Joel. "Maybe we can get whatever was out in the hallway to come and face off with us?"

Joel jutted out his chest. "Think we can't take him?"

Wade sighed and returned to working on the grate cover. He was using his Swiss Army multi-tool's screwdriver to remove one of the cover's screws. "You think it's a him?" he muttered as he worked.

"Huh?" Joel asked.

Wade got the screw out. He just had one more to go before he could push the cover aside and see if the crawl space led anywhere helpful.

"What're you doing?" Joel asked.

"I want to see where the ductwork goes," Wade said. "Maybe it leads to an exterior vent."

"Sounds like a long shot," Joel said.

Wade bristled. "Think you're going to find an exit in one of those lockers?" he snapped.

As soon as he finished talking, he heard a fingernails-on-a-chalkboard-like screech. He whirled and glared at Joel. "What're you doing now?" Wade hissed.

Joel, his dark eyes wide, shook his head. "I didn't do nothing," he whispered. Then he pointed at the wall a few feet from where Wade kneeled. "It came from over there, behind the wall."

Wade froze. He thought about the sound. Joel was right. It hadn't come from behind Wade. It had come from . . .

Wade scrambled back from the vent cover. He popped to his feet and looked around the shadowy room filled with overturned tables and chairs. The sound came again, a metal-on-metal scraping sound. It seemed to reach through the wall and carve a path across the room.

"You're probably right about the ductwork," Wade whispered, even softer than before. "Let's go check out the other storage room."

Joel didn't respond. He turned and trotted toward the door. Wade was right behind him.

Hope grasped the edge of the heavy velvet stage curtain. Its surface felt fuzzy and disconcertingly crusty against her fingers. The curtain smelled, too; the stench was acrid, and it didn't do anything to quell the nausea that had been churning in Hope's belly since they'd found the dismembered bodies in the dining room. Some of the ripped-off arms were just a few feet from the stage she and Nick stood on now. Hope shuddered and swallowed bile that gurgled up the back of her throat. She nearly squealed when Nick leaned in front of her and peered into the splotchy shadows behind the curtain.

"See anything?" he whispered.

Hope concentrated on slowing her galloping heart rate as she shook her head. "Looks like sound equipment and stage props," she whispered.

A heavy thud caused Hope and Nick to whirl around. They huddled together, staring across the dining room toward one of the party rooms.

A whispered "Sorry" followed the thud. Both Hope and Nick exhaled pent-up breath.

"It's just Adrian and Jayce," Nick said.

Hope nodded. For the hundredth time since she and the others had split up, she wished she was with Adrian. She also tried to ignore the hurt feelings that had eaten at her since Adrian had chosen Jayce as his partner.

Sure, Jayce was Adrian's best friend, but Hope, after all, was Adrian's *girlfriend*. Didn't girlfriend trump best friend?

Hope's rational side understood that Adrian's instinct was to look out for his smaller, weaker friend. He'd been doing it since he was a toddler. But it still rankled that Adrian's protective instincts placed Jayce above Hope.

When they got out of this awful place—if they got out of this awful place—Hope and Adrian were going to have a long conversation about their feelings and his priorities. Good relationships required communication; they needed to talk out their hurts instead of letting them fester.

"Come on," Nick whispered, interrupting Hope's

righteous indignation. "There might be an exit behind those wardrobes over there. We didn't look back here very thoroughly when we were running around trying to find a way out earlier."

Hope shook off her petty jealousy and looked in the direction of Nick's pointing finger. Nick was right. Three large costume wardrobes stood shoulder to shoulder toward the rear of the backstage area. It made sense that there might be a door leading to a loading dock or something back here.

Nick stepped ahead of Hope and began striding toward the wardrobes. Hope started after him, but then she stopped. A sharp tingle between her shoulder blades spun her around. She knew that sensation; she got it when she felt like she was being watched.

Hope scanned the detritus littering the dining room floor. Trying not to look too hard at the scattered body parts, she searched the shadows for movement. When she didn't see anything, she stepped through the curtain opening and dropped the curtain behind her. It was a relief to let go of the stiff fabric.

The curtain swished across the stage floor when Hope let it go; the movement sounded like a long, dry-throated sigh. The motion created a breeze, too; the air current disturbed a cluster of dust bunnies that wafted across the dusty wood floor.

Hope took a couple steps. She stopped again. The prickling feeling between her shoulder blades was now skimming down her spine and radiating throughout her body. It wasn't directional, she realized. Whatever her body was aware of wasn't necessarily behind her, but it was close by.

"Nick," Hope whispered. "Be careful."

Nick turned and winked at Hope. "That's the word of the hour, for sure."

He was right. And he was being nice. Telling him to be careful was no more helpful than telling him to breathe. They'd been nothing but careful since they'd split up from their friends. As they'd searched the kitchens, opening all the cabinets in the hope that one might be connected to a hidden corridor that led to an exit, they'd never gotten more than a couple feet apart. And without agreeing to do so, they'd stepped so lightly that their movement was nearly soundless.

Hope shook her head. "Sorry. I'm just . . ."

Nick backtracked and took Hope's hand. The warmth was familiar and welcome. She squeezed his hand to let him know she was glad he was here.

In truth, and in spite of her hurt feelings, Hope was glad to be paired with Nick. Hope and Adrian made a great couple, but they didn't yet have the connection Hope had with Nick. She and Nick had been cheerleading together for three years. They'd never considered being a couple; their link wasn't romantic. But they got each other. They were in sync. Nick was like the brother Hope didn't have.

"I get it," Nick said. "I'm scared, too."

Hope met his warm brown eyes and took comfort in his familiar rounded features. She nodded. "Okay, let's see what's behind the wardrobes."

Together, they stepped toward the tall, black-painted

cabinets. As they did, the wood floor creaked, and one of the cabinet doors fell open.

Hope sucked in her breath and tightened her grip on Nick's hand. They both froze.

Several seconds passed. Nothing inside the wardrobe moved.

Nick chuckled and gestured at the floor. "The boards are warped," he whispered. "The wardrobe doors are probably warped, too. Our weight jostled the wardrobe is all."

Hope nodded.

The pins and needles poking at her nervous system got more insistent. She turned in a full circle and searched the nooks and crannies beyond the stage props. She saw nothing that looked threatening.

Nick let go of Hope's hand. "Wow," he breathed. "Look at these." Nick strode toward the open wardrobe and flung the door back all the way.

This backstage room was poorly lit. The pale-yellow glow from half-dead stage lights high up on the wall ahead of them was spluttering as if the beams were coming from candles instead of old incandescent bulbs. Even in the uneven illumination, though, the light easily reached into the wardrobe and revealed a cluster of bright animal costumes.

Nick reached out and touched a blue bunny ear. He flicked it aside. "Whoa. This is a deep wardrobe." He leaned in farther. "I think it might have a back door. Maybe there's a secret passageway or something."

***

Jayce resisted the urge to grab on to Adrian's belt loop as he followed his friend through the hulking maze of dirty, battered arcade games. Jayce was mere inches from Adrian as he matched Adrian's pace, step for step, along the narrow aisle between a row of pinball machines and the backside of a phalanx of Skee-Ball games. Jayce's stride was so in tandem with Adrian's that their progress created what sounded like just one set of footsteps, a hushed rhythm of cautious footfalls.

Jayce had been dogging Adrian at this stuck-to-you distance ever since they'd crossed the dining room to start their search in one of the party rooms. He'd basically become an extension of Adrian, moving with him in unison as they prowled past long party tables, shoved aside boxes of party favors, and poked at vent covers in an attempt to find an exit they'd missed before. Unfortunately, neither party room revealed a way out of the building. So now they were trying to find a boarded-up window or a crawl space in the arcade area.

It was a testament to Adrian's patience that he hadn't told Jayce to back off; Jayce knew that. But he couldn't help himself. He couldn't remember ever being this frightened. And that was saying a lot. Scared was Jayce's middle name. Not really. But it might as well have been. He'd spent most of his life in a state of perpetual anxiety. Not that he wasn't entitled to his constant jitters. Being raised by a couple of obsessive perfectionists who didn't appreciate

having a nerdy artist as a son was enough to make anyone jumpy. On top of that, Jayce couldn't seem to look
and act like his peers; that made him a target for bullies and
regular kids alike, even though his best friend was one of
the popular kids. Adrian's friendship protected Jayce to
an extent, but it didn't make him bulletproof.

A muffled clank that sounded like it had come from
the stage, or near it, brought Adrian to an abrupt stop.
Jayce plowed into Adrian with an audible "oof." Adrian
turned and put a finger to his lips. Jayce nodded, but his
breathing sounded ridiculously loud. He held his breath
and listened.

Hope knew her body was trying to warn her, but because
her body didn't speak in words, she didn't fully understand what it was trying to tell her. Therefore, the warning
didn't come in time. Hope didn't realize the extent of
the danger until Nick was suddenly seized by something
unseen, something that yanked him so far into the wardrobe that he disappeared behind the faux-fur costumes.

"Nick!" Hope started toward the wardrobe, blood
pounding in her ears. She only took two steps before the
costumes churned, and Nick shot back into view.

"Nick," Hope breathed in relief.

Nick stumbled away from the wardrobe; his gaze was
locked on Hope. She met his eyes, which were bulging
and jittery.

"What . . . ?" Hope began.

Nick emitted the most deranged chuckle Hope had ever heard. He looked down. "My arm is gone." His tone was dispassionate, empty of life.

Hope shifted her gaze from Nick's face to his torso, and she immediately wondered how she could have failed to see it right away. Nick's arm *was* gone.

Hope opened her mouth to scream. She never got the sound out.

Behind Nick, the costumes seethed. Almost faster than Hope could process the movement, metal hands speared through the costumes and encircled Nick's throat.

Hope was transfixed, unable to move, even to breathe. The problem was that her brain couldn't compute something that was so not part of the world she knew.

In Hope's world, blackened metal skeletons enmeshed in tangled black wire protruding from segmented joints and pumping pistons didn't move with lightning speed. In Hope's experience, stripped-down robots with rectangular-shaped black skulls didn't leer with protruding, glowing white eyes above a gaping hinged mouth filled with huge white teeth. And in Hope's universe, sharp metal fingers didn't twist off a head with a wet snap as if it was a bottle's lid.

When Hope saw the torn remains of Nick's neck, though, she found herself in this new, appalling reality. And it annihilated her.

For several seconds, Hope could do nothing but stare into the stark black pupils gleaming in the middle of the robot's swollen white eyes. The eyes were set in metal squares and separated by a vertical swollen metal nodule that swept up to the top of the robot's skull, creating a narrow dome-like frontal "bone." This part of the robot's cranium was filthy, spotted with rust-colored stains that Hope's mind vaguely processed as dried blood. The robot's intense gaze mesmerized Hope, even as her brain fought to process the creature's existence and the bright red blood that gushed between the articulated fingers at the end of its massive metal arms.

In those few seconds, time slowed down so much that Nick's head seemed to tumble—over and over—endlessly, as it headed toward the stage floor. Hope was mesmerized by the sight of Nick's lifeless staring eyes, there and then gone, replaced by a lock of Nick's thick brown hair, slick with his blood. Then the eyes again. And then the stark white of Nick's brain stem jutting past the ragged edges of the skin at his jaw line. Rotating and falling, Nick's head arced toward the floor. And then it hit the wood with a sickening, sloppy thunk.

That's when Hope's brain rebooted. This time, it was able to get across her body's message: *Run!*

Just as the robot took a step toward her, Hope screamed. And then she took off.

Lucia and Kelly were on their way back down the main hall. Although their mission to find a way out of the pizzeria had failed, they both were in better spirits than they'd been when they'd started their search. They were even starting to joke with each other.

Maybe you should ditch Hope and hang out with me," Lucia said as they left the office that had teased them with an opening to some large ductwork but then thwarted them when they managed to get the vent cover off only to discover that the ductwork was blocked by a chunk of concrete just a few feet from its opening. No one, not even Joel, was going to get past that.

"I appreciate the way you think a lot more than she does," Lucia continued. Lucia's comment was fueled by Kelly's admission, near the start of their search, that she wanted to pair with Lucia because she admired Lucia's individuality and confidence.

Kelly laughed. Her laugh was deep and resonant, similar to her voice. Away from the others, Kelly's voice was stronger, more assertive. "You might be right," Kelly said. "Who knew so much braininess was hidden under all that hair?" She playfully flicked a couple of Lucia's curls.

Lucia grinned. And she didn't resist when Kelly took her arm as if they'd been besties forever.

It was the fear, Lucia knew. They'd been bonding because they were facing a terrifying situation together. And now they were joking because of the relief. They'd scoured their assigned area, missing not even a single square inch, and they were still alive. Again, they hadn't found a way out, but Lucia figured that being in one piece in a derelict restaurant filled with decomposing body parts and inhabited by something that had decidedly threatening footsteps was a victory worth appreciating.

"Maybe——" Lucia began.

Hope's shrill shriek cut off Lucia's words. The sound rippled through the restaurant in undulating waves.

Kelly gripped Lucia's arm so hard that her fingernails dug into Lucia's skin. Lucia and Kelly exchanged a glance and darted down the hall.

The sound was coming from the dining room. Kelly and Lucia pounded in that direction.

In just seconds, Kelly and Lucia skidded through the archway to the dining room. But they didn't get any farther.

"Run!" Hope screamed as she careened toward them. Waving her arms toward the hallway Lucia and Kelly had just come down, Hope yelled, "Go! Go!"

Lucia and Kelly didn't balk. Immediately, they turned and retraced their steps. Hope caught up with them and they all ran together.

Out of the corner of her eye, Lucia saw Adrian and Jayce tear out of the arcade. They galloped toward the archway.

"What is it?" Adrian called out as they came.

Hope didn't answer. She just raced, pell-mell, any vestige of her cheerleading grace gone, down the hall. Everyone else followed her.

When they were just a few feet down the hall, Joel and Wade surged through a doorway on the left side of the hall, opposite the door to the office. They thundered toward the rest of the group. "What the hell?" Joel bellowed as they came.

Hope skidded to a stop outside the men's restroom.

She looked around wildly. Her face was so white it was practically translucent. Her eyes were red. Tears streaked her smudged cheeks.

When she spotted Adrian, Hope cried out and lunged for him. She threw herself at him, and he wrapped her in his arms.

"Shh," Adrian soothed. "Shh. It's okay. Tell me what happened."

Hope said something, but the words were so entangled in hiccupping sobs that they weren't decipherable. Her chest heaved as she pressed against Adrian as if she could disappear into him.

Lucia rotated to be sure nothing was coming down the hall toward them, from either direction. Then she looked at the others. She frowned.

"Uh, where's Nick?" Lucia asked.

Hope let out a wail, and her legs went out from under her. Adrian caught her and lifted her, cradling her like a baby.

Hope began babbling again. Everyone leaned in to try to understand her.

Lucia's stomach roiled. Tremors cascaded through her body, chilling her, and they brought with them a miserable knowing that she tried to deny.

The denial lasted not even a half second. In that time, Hope's words took form.

"He's dead," Hope burbled. "Nick's dead."

Everyone exchanged disbelieving looks. They all looked up and down the hallway.

"What—" Joel began.

Adrian cut him off. "We can't stand out in the open like this."

As if to affirm his statement, a long grinding noise resounded through the building. Its origin was impossible to determine. It seemed to come from everywhere at once.

"Come on," Lucia said. "The Parts and Service Room is filled with metal parts. If we hide in there, we can find something to use as a weapon."

Adrian, his face hard, nodded once.

As a group, they all scurried down the hall toward the open doorway to the Parts and Service Room. It took only seconds for all of them to rush through the door. Wade was the last one through. He immediately slammed the door and locked it.

As soon as he did, Hope spoke. "I'm okay," she said. "I can stand."

Adrian gazed at her with concern, and he set her down. She gripped his arm, but she remained upright.

As soon as they were locked in the room, Lucia regretted her suggestion. Yes, the room was filled with metal that could be used as weapons, but the room was also creepy in the extreme. Its lighting, already spotty when Lucia and Kelly had explored it earlier, was now flickering as if struggling to stay on. The overhead bulbs' unsteady illumination did little to relieve the room's spook factor.

Crammed full of animatronic suits and robotic endoskeletons, the room was set up like a beauty shop for robots. It contained three metal chairs complete with clamps—the chairs could have doubled for torture devices. The chairs were flanked by a couple of workbenches strewn with robotic parts. The suits, rigid and upright, stood around the periphery of the room, making it appear as if a dozen or so Freddy Fazbear characters were surrounding them. Lucia *knew* that the suits were empty. She and Kelly had checked them all—none contained the endoskeletons necessary to animate them. Still the suits' staring white eyes and open mouths looked way too lifelike.

"What happened to Nick?" Adrian asked. The timbre of his words was calm and soft, as if he was pacifying a cornered animal.

Hope responded to his soothing demeanor. Licking her lips, she blinked a couple times. Then she started talking in a flat tone, her words slow and measured, seemingly emotionless. But Lucia knew the emptiness was a facade. Emotions Hope couldn't process yet bubbled below her stiff recitation of the facts.

"We were looking behind the curtains, in the flickering room," Hope said. "Nick thought there might be a hidden exit at the back of some wardrobes. I was nervous. Something didn't feel right. But I didn't say anything. Then it came out of the wardrobe. It shot out so fast that it didn't seem real. It took his arm and then it took him by the neck. It grabbed his neck. It ripped his head off."

When Hope stopped speaking, the only thing Lucia could hear was the combined sound of everyone's breathing. Hope had stopped crying. Her face was slack. She was staring at one of the endoskeletons.

Hope was in shock. Obviously.

"What was it?" Jayce asked. His voice cracked in the middle of the question.

"It was big and metal and shiny and black," Hope said. "A skeleton, but not a skeleton. Awful eyes. Massive teeth. Filthy. Covered in dried blood."

Everyone frowned at her.

Kelly reached out and took Hope's hand. "Hope, we don't understand. Can you tell us more?"

Hope shook her head, but she pointed. They all turned and looked at one of the endoskeletons propped against the wall.

"It was that, only bigger," Hope said.

Lucia stared at the endoskeleton. Then she turned and looked at all the animatronic suits. Her heart lurched up into her throat.

Hope kept staring at the endoskeleton. As she did, her breathing quickened, and she began to back away from it.

Lucia kept looking at the animatronic suits that surrounded them. She was sure that everyone could hear the throbbing of her heart, which sounded to her ears like a huge bass drum being pounded faster and faster and faster.

When Kelly and Lucia had searched this room, the animatronic suits had been empty. But how long had they all been in the hallway? They'd been so concerned about Hope, so stupefied by her story, Lucia had no idea how much time had passed.

Hope licked her lips so she could get out the idea tha

had formed, horribly, in her mind. "What if," she began, "an endoskeleton could get into costumes like this?" She gestured at the animatronic suits.

Everyone turned and looked at the dusty characters. Lucia's gaze shifted to each one in turn. She studied a goofy critter dressed in green overalls, a sly-looking orange cat, and a huge gray dog with purple, poodle-like scruff on top of its head and around its neck, wrists, and ankles. Next to the poodle-like dog, and behind Hope, was another dog, its lolling tongue giving it a friendly look in spite of its spiked collar.

As Lucia studied it, the dog moved. And the already struggling light bulbs gave out. Hope squealed as soon as the room went black. One of the guys grunted.

Then the lights were back on. They were still weak, unstable, but they were on.

In the moment the lights came on, in that fraction of a second, the floppy-eared dog stepped forward, and its arms came up. It grabbed Hope's biceps just as Lucia cried, "Look out!"

Lucia's warning was worthless. By the time she got the words out, the thing in the suit had already torn Hope's arms from her body.

Hope shrieked so loudly that her scream felt like it was coming from inside Lucia. The sound was an endless keen of indescribable pain and shock. It careened around the room, assaulting them with the desperate finality of what was happening.

As the scream coursed around them, the homicidal thing grabbed Hope's torso, flipped her upside down, and wrenched her legs free of her hips. Hope's scream crescendoed to an impossibly high octave. And it continued to drill into Lucia's ears as the Freddy thing once again inverted Hope's body before grabbing her head and wresting it from her neck.

The screaming stopped abruptly.

In the sucking silence that followed, Lucia noticed wet warmth on her face and arms. She felt the stickiness that was gluing her shirt to her body. She looked down. She was drenched in Hope's blood.

And so was everyone else.

For two long seconds, no one moved. They all stared at the carnage that used to be Hope. Adrian's eyes were locked on the vacant gaze of Hope's disembodied head.

Then Kelly took Lucia's hand. "Come on," she shouted.

Lucia stumbled as Kelly tugged her toward the door. There, they fell into Joel, who was scrabbling to get the door unlocked.

Behind them, the heavy tapping footsteps that were now all too familiar started their way. Lucia wanted to cover her ears so she couldn't hear the hiss and rasp that paired with the taps.

Joel got the door open, and he tore through it. The others scrambled after him.

They bolted, as one, down the hall.